John F Plimmer's

The Pie Man

Another thriller in the Victorian Detective's series featuring Richard Rayner of Scotland Yard

Copyright © 2019 John Plimmer
All rights reserved.
ISBN: 978-1-7974-3582-4

To Roger Baker – the man who crossed me over the street and is my greatest literary supporter

'It is not from the tall crowded workhouse of prosperity that men first or clearest see the eternal stars of heaven'
Theodore Parker

'Please sir, I want some more'
Charles Dickens

Chapter One

His eight-year old world had become a vacuum of darkness visited only by pain and guilt since God had taken his beloved mother out of his life to sit with the angels in Heaven. Or so she had so amorously told him, with the love only a mother could bestow upon her own child. And yet, his loneliness demanded she remained close to him, if only to be permanently lodged within his infantile imagination. Convinced his mother remained at his side, the isolated and vulnerable young boy refused to accept the only person who had ever truly loved him, had abandoned her fragile son. The young and innocent Thomas Wake could face up to almost any ordeal as long she was there, watching over him; advising him; still soothing his hardships and tortuous pains with her paternal love.

Even as the insipid looking boy stared through watery eyes beyond the large classroom window, his mother was there;

standing at the bottom of the garden; still smiling reassuringly. He followed her gentle and loving stare towards two black ravens pecking at each other in a feathered confrontation to decide which one would be allowed to remain on top of the nearby roughly hewn brick wall. Oh yes, his beloved mama had most definitely remained at his side.

"It's time Tommy to return to your seat," she softly said, the calmness of her words reaching out to him from where she stood.

"I will mama," he quietly answered, turning to look back at the empty spacious classroom before his feeble and spindly legs carried him back to where he had been ordered to remain seated by the Mistress, Mrs. Grimbold. It was then his courage abandoned him, together with the disappearance of his mother's apparition. He sat with his young head resting on both arms, weeping tears which had become ever present since she had passed on.

"Oh, why did you leave me mama?" he cried out, as the pain of loneliness once again returned. Although her explanation had been convincing when telling him that everyone would eventually be called to help God in His Kingdom, the Master, Mr. Grimbold had bluntly told young Tom that his mother had been taken by the Cholera. How could an eight-year old child be expected to know what the Cholera was? Thomas Wake certainly didn't.

Mrs. Grimbold, the Mistress of the Workhouse, had strictly ordered the lad to remain sitting, until she fetched her husband to decide what further punishment should be added to his already tortured and dire, meaningless existence. Unlike his mother, she only embraced him with cold, harsh words and well-rehearsed revulsion at his mere presence. He only felt hatred towards her. Mrs. Grimbold was a witch who one day, when the emaciated boy had become a man of enormous strength and power, he would return and set the wicked woman alight with a torch, laughing as he watched her burn in the flames. But then the series of imaginative episodes from which he drew some comfort evaporated. The sound of echoing footsteps could be heard approaching the classroom door.

A pouted pale face masked by tears turned to look towards the door at the far end. They were coming to deal with him yet again, only too willing to subject the helpless victim to what would be a prolonged bout of the harshest and most cruel form of so-called discipline imaginable, short of taking away his life. But that had always been the case, even when his mother had been alive at his side to watch over him. The boy had rejected the vociferous claims that he was a weakling; a wretched thief;

an unwanted scoundrel; a discarded dilberry, and all the other hurtful names thrown his way.

Then there had been the frequent lashings with their severe cutting pain and scars, and the freezing cold concrete slabs down in the rat-infested coal cellar he was made to lie on. The tortuous burning of the whip marks across his young back still remained raw. His new guardians had often justified their immense cruelty by telling the boy it was all necessary discipline, inflicted for his own good to help him develop into a responsible citizen later in his life. And yet he could never understand what he had done wrong to deserve such primitive punishment, or warrant the severity of that which reduced him to a confused wreck of a mere child. His mother used to tell him to have faith, as it was far better they remained under that roof than be cast out on to the streets, but he remained unconvinced.

"Here's the wretch," the skinny, pale looking woman with the fearsome staring eyes called out, as both she and her husband entered the classroom and approached the boy who was far from being an insubordinate child.

"Well boy, what have you to say for yourself," the Master bawled at the youngster. Mr. Grimbold appeared to be enormous to the small and fragile Thomas Wake, a man whose eyes weren't as cruel as his wife's but with a voice which vibrated around the room, sufficient to send chills up any boys' spine, if any other boy was present that is. How strange it was, no other child was ever present when sentence was about to be pronounced.

"Well sir..." young Thomas quietly spoke, before surrendering to the enormity of the circumstances and retreating back into silence.

"Bah, the cat's got his tongue. Tell me again Mrs. Grimbold what this heathen of a scallywag has been up to."

"I've already told you Mr. Grimbold, he was caught by Mrs. Graham stealing milk from the kitchen," the Mistress said, referring to the head cook.

"Very well, let's not dilly and dally any longer. Prepare yourself boy. You know the penalty for stealing." There it was; the inevitable; the presence of the birch being held tightly in one fat and hairy hand.

In a last desperate attempt to mitigate his position, Thomas pleaded, "I only had one drink sir because I was thirsty."

"It's still larceny boy and you know the consequences. Prepare yourself."

Not requiring any instruction or guidance, the child dropped his rumpled trousers and having repeated the same posture on numerous occasions previously, leant over one of the desks, quivering like a petrified spectacle of human naivety.

The whip-like sound of the Master's cane pierced through the air and cut sharply into the boy's buttocks, causing the refractory infant to cry out. Only, Thomas Wake was not a refractory infant. The same punishment was repeated several times until there were no more tears to be shed, and he was on the verge of losing consciousness. He was yanked off the desk top like a rag doll by the Mistress and ordered to pull up his trousers. The boy was in agony and stood straight, like a lost soul in purgatory, still grimacing from the fires blazing across his rear end. Thomas knew that wouldn't be the end of his ordeal and anticipated other ways of so called, 'correction', about to be inflicted upon his fragile body.

"Two nights in the cellar will give you time to consider your criminal behaviour my boy," Mr. Grimbold declared, bullishly, "And I warn you now, one more repeat of this felony or any other fall from grace and you will be thrown out onto the streets." At that, the Master turned and left without saying another word. His merciless spouse remained for a few moments longer, enthralled by the sight of such terror and pain standing before her, and displaying a mischievous smile as rare as a Royal visit from the

Queen herself.

After taking her fill of what to normal people would have been viewed as an obscenity, she grabbed the orphan by his collar, forcibly dragging him down two flights of steps into the darkness. The coal cellar door was jerked open and the young captive was violently flung on to the icy cold floor. His nightmare had returned with a vengeance. His tears were in full flow and he glanced up to see the last glimpse of light disappear as the door was banged shut to the sound of a heavy bolt being pushed across. Thomas could see nothing and the air in which he lay was filled with coal dust, making him cough each time he drew breath. Emotional tears and a burning throat were Thomas Wake's unjustified lot.

The silence was formidable except for the sound of rats scurrying across the floor, encouraging the eight-year old to stand and lean against one of the walls. The boy was unable to sit down on the hard, solid floor as a result of the thrashing he'd received. Thomas stood for some considerable time, his only comfort being his mother's memory which at least eased away some of the intense pain he was feeling from the hot coals racing to and fro across his buttocks. His beloved mama had told him to always look to the future. What future? How could he ever escape the cruel clutches of the Grimbolds?

There was no natural light in the cellar, just a closed trap door in the ceiling for bags of coal to be thrown through. There was no way the young miscreant could see whether it was day time or night time outside, but didn't really care, having succumbed to total apathy. After a while, various objects began to take shape in the darkness, as his eyes began to adapt. The stricken unfortunate could make out a pile of coal in one corner with a large shovel resting nearby against a wall. He could see a bucket positioned near to where he stood, and was becoming accustomed to the small furry things chasing around his feet. There were scars on his skinny legs where he'd been bitten before by vermin so many times.

As the hours passed by, his young mind roamed across the short history of his life span, and he wondered whether the same treatment he was subjected to at the workhouse was inflicted on other children. It did appear that he was the only inmate who spent time in this frightful cellar. His deep-seated thoughts were interrupted by the barely audible sound of the bolt being drawn back on the other side of the door. He braced himself, fearful that Mrs. Grimbold had returned to punish him further for some other innocuous error he'd been found to have committed. He relaxed, as the door slowly opened and his visitor became visible.

Nelly Pritchard, who was one of the upstairs maids, appeared holding a dimmed lantern to her face, allowing the boy to see her lift a finger to her mouth, before sidling across to where he was standing. The tears began to flow again and he looked up at the young lady in desperate need of comfort.

"Now, now, Tommy, you must be brave. All of this will soon go away, I promise," she said, placing a loving arm around his fragile shoulders. He buried his dirty face into her bosom and continued to quietly weep. The woman did nothing to stop him, overwhelmed by the harsh cruelty this young wretch was again being made to suffer.

When the boy's sobbing began to ease, she gave him one final and gently hug, before looking into his face. She knew there was little time as she glanced across at the partially open door, reassuring herself that the Mistress was not present.

"I've brought you something to cool your wounds," she whispered, handing a small jar to him which contained ointment.

"Drop your trousers Tommy and I'll put some on for you, and then when the stinging returns put more on yourself."

The young lady, who had helped the lad on a number of occasions, did as she had promised, bringing instant relief to his discomfort. Nelly Pritchard abhorred the kind of violence which, in her view was too readily dished out by the husband and wife partnership responsible for the workhouse. But she wouldn't dare make any complaint, desperately needing to retain her position and in the knowledge, it would most definitely come to an abrupt end should she let her inner feelings be known.

"Be brave young sir and try and get some sleep. Lie on your side and use these for bedding," she said, lifting a couple of empty sacks off the floor, "They will help you to keep warm and it won't be long before they let you out. If you are still here tomorrow, don't worry yourself, I shall return and bring you something else to eat and drink." She then handed him a wrapped-up parcel of cheese and bread, and a small bottle of water, taken from a basket she had with her.

The maid had known the boy's mother and had admired the way in which the woman had worked long hours with nothing inside her, knitting and stitching for what mere pittance was placed in her hands in return only to catch a disease which eventually took her life. Thomas's mother had sworn that one day she would have saved enough for both of them to leave the workhouse and live like normal human beings. Alas, that particular dream had disappeared together with her own demise.

By the time Nelly had reached the door, the young alleged refractory was already devouring the cheese and bread and she smiled before leaving, quietly replacing the bolt on the other side.

Thanks to the kindness of one individual lady, the youngster managed to sleep throughout the remainder of that night, occasionally awaking as a result of the cold and interference from the other occupants of the cellar. Of course, he knew that in Nellie Pritchard he had a friend, one who was doing her utmost to look after him in whatever way she could. But she wasn't his mother, and he was still pining for the only woman he had ever loved and who had loved him unconditionally. During his waking hours, the eight-year old concentrated his mind on creating hypothetical situations, although perhaps not so hypothetical. He pictured himself charging up to the front door of the workhouse and demanding that both Mr. and Mrs. Grimbold pay homage to him by saying how sorry they were for having inflicted such misery upon him. Then he would have them flogged before incarcerating them in a far-away dungeon for the remainder of their lives. Then his mother's face would reappear and she would be shaking her head and wagging a gentle finger to tell him to be more charitable. Such hallucinations didn't prevent him however, from scheming and planning ways in which he would eventually seek his revenge. But, before that, there was another mission he would have to fulfil - to find his younger sister, Emily. She often visited his nightmares, living in the same conditions as himself and being made to suffer in a similar way.

In reality, the young Thomas Wake was still to face a long and painful road ahead of him before reaching maturity. He would be moved from one workhouse to another as an orphan, and would approach adult life after having become acquainted with most of the Corrective Institutions in and around London.

In the years to follow, he would never forget the cold darkness of that cellar, or the thrashings and occasional other beatings he was subjected to at the hands of the Grimbolds. But he would never again be forced to endure such constant depraved atrocities with other Masters and Mistresses, where-ever he found himself lodging and working to survive. But for now, the boy was going nowhere.

Chapter Two

The architectural magnificence of the newly constructed Royal Albert Hall stood out against the night sky in all of its lavish grandeur, beckoning the excited and fascinated hordes of invited guests through the main entrance doors, into its awe-inspiring interior.

Richard Rayner stood with his wife, Clarice, gazing up at the mosaic frieze surrounding the building, explaining the significance of various tiles representing the arts and sciences.

"You can see dear, how the designers have created buff figures outlined in black on a chocolate background. They represent sixteen different allegorical groups within the complete mosaic."

"I will take your word for it, Richard," she politely answered, "But I do find the whole structure extremely grandiose and remarkable in its achievement."

He turned to look at what he regarded as being his wife's

natural beauty, and remarked, "Let's hope the gifted Richard Wagner views the building in the same light. I'm sure his opera will compliment such a grandiose and remarkable structure, as you so rightly describe it." He then paused to look beyond the other patrons surrounding where they stood, and enquired, "I wonder if the Superintendent and Henry have arrived yet?"

The Rayners' had taken advantage of Frederick Morgan's generous offer of sharing four additional tickets, benevolently placed into the Superintendent's hands with the compliments of the Commissioner. It wasn't every evening an opportunity came, whereby they could attend one of eight concerts being performed at the Hall under the personal attention of the celebrated German composer, Richard Wagner. The remaining two tickets had been allocated to the Inspector's Sergeant, Henry Bustle, who had reluctantly accepted them, his knowledge of Wagner and the Opera being somewhat limited and yet acknowledging it was an opportunity to take his wife, Nellie, to the theatre at the least expense.

Being a confirmed bachelor, Frederick Morgan attended the event alone, but was excitedly gleaming when he first set eyes on Richard and Clarice Rayner, as they took their seats next to him in one of the upper balconies. The Superintendent was a short, well-built Welshman from Porthcawl with a head covered in red hair cut short. He lived alone in his own house in Bermondsey and frequently portrayed the kind of self-disciplined man he in fact was, having been a major in the Coldstream Guards. Yet beneath all the wind and bluster was an individual who had a charitable side to his character, hence the sharing out of the concert tickets.

He welcomed his first two guests to arrive and explained that he hoped to personally meet with the maestro himself backstage after the concert was over.

"I'm sure your charming wife would wish to join us Rayner," he said, looking all around for his first glimpse of Henry Bustle and his spouse, who he was concerned might miss the first curtain.

"I would love to meet the composer," Clarice answered, with a hint of exhilaration in her voice, "Would it really be possible; I know so little about his work."

"He owns his own theatre in Bayreuth, Germany," Morgan explained, "And is known for his powerfully dramatic operas which have given him well deserved acclaim throughout the civilised world."

"I also believe our Mr. Wagner is a somewhat controversial

figure as a result of his hostile and anti-Semitic works," Rayner pointed out, failing to pour cold water on his wife's joyful anticipation, "He certainly appears to make a number of political statements in many of his compositions."

"Is that really important Richard?" his companion for the evening answered, "Master Wagner does appear to be an interesting man nevertheless." Clarice then turned to Frederick Morgan and confessed, "I had no idea you were interested in opera Superintendent."

"I find they invigorate me Mrs. Rayner and of all the composers, Wagner is amongst my favourites."

"Have you a preferred Opera?"

"The one we are about to see my dear," Morgan answered with genuine testimony, "Der Fliegende Holländer, or in English, The Flying Dutchman."

"It is a story about a sea captain who is cursed to sail forever for blasphemy," Richard Rayner quietly and respectfully explained to his wife, "It is a love story in which the captain's redemption can only be achieved by the love of a faithful woman."

When it came to knowing a little about everything, there was nothing disclosed by her intellectual husband which surprised Clarice and she asked, "Have you seen it before Richard?"

"Yes my dear, when at Oxford I recall seeing The Flying Dutchman performed in one act by an amateur theatre group." Rayner was referring to that period of his young life spent as a student of mathematics at Oxford, before he joined the Metropolitan Police.

"In fact, it was initially written by Wagner with the intention of being played in one continuous act, but do not fret Mrs. Rayner, it has been divided into three separate acts for this evening's performance," Morgan explained, "Ah, I see the Commissioner and his party have arrived." The Superintendent was looking across at one of the boxes near to the Royal box, not far from where they were seated, which also held Richard Rayner's attention as he watched Sir Edmund Henderson busily showing the various members of his party to their seats.

Then the orchestra fell silent, signalling the end of their tuning up period and communicating an unspoken invitation for the audience to settle down in anticipation of the commencement of the evening's entertainment. As the lights inside the auditorium dimmed, there was a slight disturbance to Morgan and Rayner's right. The sight of Nellie Bustle leading her husband along the row of seats until reaching where their friends were seated, was a relief to the others. There was a distinct look of guilt on the Sergeant's face, but his wife looked radiant and sat next to Clarice, smiling and looking charming. She was a few years older than Mrs. Rayner but frequently displayed the same youthful aura, most certainly looking younger than her years, which was a sure sign of happy and contented matrimony.

Henry Bustle whispered his apologies and Rayner looked at him in surprise, not because the couple had almost missed the beginning of the First Act, but because never before had he seen his Sergeant looking so smartly attired. Bustle did look somewhat out of place however, with a collar and bow tie around his neck; the Detective Inspector assumed this had been the result of a great deal of attention from his wife.

Finally, and following the usual short silent period of anticipation after members of the audience had taken their seats, the great composer appeared on centre stage, welcomed by tumultuous applause. Frederick Morgan couldn't control his admiration and stood putting his hands loudly together. Such an act triggered the occupants of every row behind them having to stand to keep the composer in their sights.

Wilhelm Richard Wagner bowed deeply to the audience before

turning and stepping over to the lectern. Raising the baton in one hand, he allowed it to hover tantalisingly in the air before thrusting it downwards with purpose, to signal an overwhelming trumpet fanfare. The Great Wagner Festival had begun and the audience sat mesmerised by the loud dramatic music and impressive acts which followed.

Whilst Henry Bustle was thinking only of the possibility of visiting a public house before closing time and drinking his fill of black ale, everyone else in the building was entranced by the impact being made upon them by the musical scores and songs bellowing out from the stage. It was indeed, a series of moving recitals and awe-inspiring music. On one occasion, both Nellie Bustle and Clarice Rayner had tears in their eyes, as the artist playing Wagner's sea captain met the woman who was to redeem him with her love. By the time the interval came the Royal Albert Hall was filled with unabated emotion.

Refreshments were served and the small group made their way out into an adjoining corridor which was illumined by gas lamps attached to the walls.

People gathered in small groups; all conversing, with some laughing aloud, but mostly expressing their views on what the first half of the concert had meant to them. Frederick Morgan wasted little time in putting a light to his pipe of tobacco, which had an odour not unpleasant, surprising both Rayner and Bustle, having been used to an obnoxious smell coming from the same pipe when their Superintendent indulged himself during working hours at Scotland Yard.

"What do you think of it so far ladies?" the senior detective enquired.

"I'm not sure if I fully understood everything that took place," Nellie Bustle confessed, "But I managed to follow most of it, and certainly recognise a pulsating and emotional role played when I see one. I thought the sea captain was captivating."

"And what of you Mrs. Rayner, is this the first occasion you have attended the Opera?"

"Yes, it is Superintendent and I have thoroughly enjoyed it so far. I must admit to becoming a little emotional when the captain first met the woman who he falls in love with. It reminded me so much of how myself and Richard first met," she said, teasing her husband who blushed slightly, feeling a little embarrassed.

There was no doubting though that the most enthusiastic in the small group of patrons was the Superintendent, and he continued conversing with a glint in his eye. He made no attempt to conceal the admiration he was feeling towards the evening's entertainment thus far. There was no doubting his amour for the Opera, which had come as a surprise to everyone else, and resembled a child opening its presents on Christmas morning, dazzled by their contents.

"What a splendid and enthralling evening," he said to no one in particular.

Richard Rayner also remained looking as if he was savouring the moment, as if analysing every tiny part of the performance as he would do so when solving a mathematical problem. However, poor Henry Bustle couldn't avoid a bemused look on his face, edging towards excruciating boredom and standing there with a finger constantly visiting the inside of his collar, obviously feeling some irritation around his oversized neck.

They were then unexpectedly joined by the Commissioner, Sir Edmund Henderson, who was immediately introduced to the two ladies by Frederick Morgan.

"We have Sir Edmund to thank for being given the opportunity to feast our eyes on such a magnificent spectacle," the Superintendent explained, being a little over the top, or so Rayner thought, realising for the first time just how obsessed his senior was with both Wagner and his magnum opus.

"Well now, if at the end of the final act you remain so

enthusiastic, perhaps you ladies would care to join us backstage and meet the great composer in person. You would be most warmly welcomed," Sir Edmund invited, procuring encouraging nods of the head from both Clarice and Nellie. He was a well-built man who stood with a straight back with white hair and mutton chop whiskers which added to his look of distinction.

"Please enjoy the remainder of the entertainment and I look forward to meeting you again a little later." The Commissioner smiled, before turning and making his exit, leaving an initial impressionable perception on the two ladies in particular.

"What a nice gentleman," Nellie Bustle remarked, after the Head of the Metropolitan Police had disappeared.

"He'll do for us," Morgan answered, abruptly and with genuine sincerity.

"We are fortunate to have him," Richard Rayner commented, "Sir Edmund is a very understanding man who doesn't suffer fools gladly, would you agree Henry?" he offered, trying to bring the Sergeant into the conversation.

"Yes sir, which is surprising for a man with such a distinctive military background."

"He was in the army before he joined the police then?" his wife enquired.

"Yes madam," Morgan confirmed, "Sir Edmund was an officer in the Royal Engineers." The Superintendent was about to enlarge on both his own and the Commissioner's military careers when the call was made for the patrons to return to their seats, as the second half of the evening's entertainment was about to commence.

The lights in the auditorium had once again dimmed by the time they had settled back in their seats, only to be greeted by the main attraction who stood facing the audience from the centre of the stage.

"Thank you for such a wonderful and warm reception you have given us all this evening," Richard Wagner acknowledged, before bowing his head and receiving yet another outburst of applause from the floor. For a man heading towards the twilight of his life, he certainly made an imposing figure standing up there in the lights coming from rows of bright lanterns hidden from the audience.

"Because I am no longer as young as I used to be, I find myself forced to recruit the assistance of younger men."

His audience laughed in response.

"Therefore, it gives me the greatest of pleasure to introduce my countryman and fellow composer who has journeyed all the way from Germany to attend this evenings performance. Please welcome Herr Gerhard Richter to whom I shall hand over the baton."

More loud applause followed and Frederick Morgan was back on his feet for the second time that night, clapping his hands together in recognition of the enormous amount of idol worshipping respect he held for the famous composer. All eyes watched as Wagner then stepped across the stage to the far end, before sitting down in a large armchair and remaining there throughout the remainder of the evening's entertainment.

The second half of the concert was as pulsating and entertaining as the first, and following the conclusion of the final act, artists and musicians took their bows behind both Wagner and Richter to cheers and even louder applause than before. The lights came up and the audience began to move towards the exit doors, the rows of seats having disgorged their occupants in an orderly fashion. It was then that a sudden shock wave swept through the crowds still waiting to leave, resulting in everyone's head turning up towards one of the vacated boxes.

The sound of a high-pitched scream filled the auditorium and a female member of staff appeared with both hands up against her petrified face. The young girl stared down at those below with eyes filled with terror and excitedly shrieked, "There's been a murder, a horrible, horrible murder."

They were all jolted into sudden panic and despair, except the three detectives who gazed across at one another in disbelief. The same girl who had just brought a successful night at the Opera to a dramatic ending, fainted.

Chapter Three

For a fleeting few seconds blip, as though time itself had stopped momentarily, the onlookers froze where they stood, including the three gentlemen from Scotland Yard and the two ladies. All eyes watched as two male members of staff appeared in the same box occupied by the girl who had fainted, and could be seen to carefully carry her away.

Just as if he was bidding farewell to his local tobacconist, Frederick Morgan turned and tipped his hat at Clarice Rayner and Nellie Bustle, requesting they remain where they were, "Until we can be assured there is no danger ladies," he explained.

"We face danger every time we walk along a street Superintendent," Clarice Rayner snapped back, but her husband immediately made his presence known, imploring his wife to stay where she was for a short time, not wanting her to be in the way.

He could see by the expression on Clarice's face, she was not impressed by the suggestion but for the sake of maintaining a peaceful existence, bowed her head in mock obedience.

"Right lads, let's be off and see what all this bleedin' lot is about," Morgan confidently directed, moving his rounded torso out of the aisle and heading towards where he could gain access to the upper tier. His two detectives followed, leaving the ladies behind.

All three followed the ongoing rumpus until reaching a small gentleman's smoking room in a communal corridor. Employees of the Royal Albert Hall stood quietly appearing inadequate, confused and completely unhinged. It was left to Henry Bustle to endeavour to restore some semblance of normality and harmonious order back into their lives, whilst Morgan and Rayner stepped inside the room.

The scene which greeted the two senior detectives was slouched down in one of the arm chairs near to the far wall. It was the lifeless body of a man, heavily built with grey wavy hair, wearing evening dress and staring back at them. Blood flowed down the front of the victims white starched shirt and an initial observation led the detectives to suspect he had been stabbed to death. Strangely though, some bruising was also visible below the left eye and near to the corner of a thick-lipped gaping mouth. There was also a perfumed odour in the room, different from the prominent smell of tobacco smoke.

A distressed young lady was standing outside in the corridor with other members of the Hall staff. She was uncontrollably sobbing with a young male attendant supporting her shoulder. When asked for her name by Henry Bustle, the upset waitress, who was wearing a smart black uniform and frilly white apron, confirmed she was Mary Marchant and was employed as a catering assistant at the Royal Albert Hall.

The Sergeant was continuing to make some initial notes when two constables appeared, having been summoned from outside by other members of staff. Upon seeing the Superintendent and Inspector in attendance, they stood awaiting further instruction.

"Was it you who found the body?" Bustle enquired.

"Yes," Miss Marchant whispered, "I was checking to make sure no one was left inside the smoking room after the final curtain. It was horrible with all that blood."

"Was anyone else with you?" the Sergeant asked, looking at the young man who was supporting the lady.

"No, I was on my own which made it worse."

"Did you see anyone enter or leave the room?"

"Not after everyone left following the intermission."

"Very well my dear, if I could have your address someone will call and see you tomorrow to take your statement. In the meantime, I suggest you go home and try and get some rest. You have been through quite an horrendous ordeal," he advised paternally.

Richard Rayner appeared in the doorway of the smoking room and immediately directed one of the constables to summon more help from Scotland Yard.

"Henry, I want you to visit St Mary's Hospital and seek out Doctor Critchley and bring him back here." Rayner was referring to the pathologist who had worked with the detectives on numerous previous investigations.

Satisfied he'd set the right wheels in motion, the Inspector rejoined Frederick Morgan, who he found standing over a table beneath which the deceased man's legs were outstretched. Smoking a small cigar, the Superintendent was staring at an untouched pastry pie which was sitting on the table top.

"It appears our man never got the opportunity to eat his supper, Inspector," Morgan remarked.

"If that's what indeed it was."

"Well, somebody's tried to take a bite, there's teeth marks on the one side."

Rayner began to search through the pockets of the victim's jacket pulling out an address card.

"It would appear his name is, Claude Grimbold and he is connected in some way to the Upper Clapton Workhouse."

"Bleedin' hell Rayner, what would he be doing at a Wagner concert?"

"That's for us to find out Superintendent. Might I suggest you leave this with me for now and go and join the backstage party. I know how much you have been looking forward to meeting Mr. Wagner and it might still not be too late."

As he spoke, Sir Edmund Henderson arrived and requested an initial briefing, which Morgan gave to him, sharing what little knowledge they had gained so far.

"Very well, I'm sure we can leave this in Inspector Rayner's capable hands Frederick, so come and meet the great composer himself," the Commissioner suggested, before leaving with the Superintendent hot on his heels, like an infant about to come face to face with the Tooth Fairy for the very first time.

Rayner promptly returned to the task of searching the victims clothing, but found nothing else of interest. After a short while his wife, Clarice appeared, explaining that Nellie Bustle had gone with the Commissioner and Superintendent backstage.

"Why didn't you go with them Clarice?" Rayner asked, "It would be the opportunity of a lifetime to meet Richard Wagner in person."

"My place is with my husband Richard, that's all that matters. Do you know who this poor man is yet?"

Rayner shared the victim's identity with her, before suddenly being struck by an idea. It was an extremely doubtful idea but needed to be investigated whilst participants involved in the earlier concert still remained inside the Hall. He told the remaining constable to admit no one into the room and to ensure the door was kept secured until he returned.

"You might yet meet the famous composer," he then suggested to his wife, "And manage to remain at your husband's side at the same time."

The reception room was larger and more spacious than either of them could have possibly imagined, and Richard Wagner could be seen standing at the far end with a queue of dignitaries waiting to make the great composer's acquaintance. Rayner could see the Commissioner and his small party standing busy chatting away, with Frederick Morgan and Nellie Bustle amongst them.

"Stay close to my side," the Inspector suggested to his wife, before taking off, weaving his way through the excited crowd, which contained some of London's wealthiest men and their ladies.

Verbal pleasantries and ingratiating looks were replaced by stern faces and inquisitive eyes, as the couple made their way directly towards where the German composer was standing. The renowned visitor to London was surrounded by a few of those members of the management team responsible for the evening's entertainment. Richard Wagner was making himself available to as many people as possible, and seemingly enjoying the accolades being bestowed upon him.

Rayner pushed his way through with Clarice clinging on to the back of his jacket, until he was within a few feet of his subject.

"Herr Wagner," he called out, slightly breathless.

The famous man turned to look at the tall, slim dark-haired intruder with the handsome features, at first looking somewhat perplexed.

"I am Inspector Richard Rayner from Scotland Yard and I am investigating a murder which has unfortunately just taken place inside this building. Could I have a few words with you sir in private?"

The composer smiled and quietly answered in a deep voice, "Only if you apologise immediately Inspector for spoiling my party."

"Then if that what it takes sir, I apologise," Rayner said insincerely and bowing his head.

"Very well, perhaps there is somewhere more private in which I can converse with the Inspector, Master Franklin," Wagner spoke, directing his words at a much smaller, middle-aged gentleman standing nearby and who was obviously one of the officials responsible for supervising the activities inside the reception room. In fact, Rayner later learned the same man was the general manager of the Royal Albert Hall.

Superintendent Frederick Morgan watched from close by with a certain degree of puzzlement, as Mr. and Mrs. Rayner were escorted by both the composer and manager away from the assembly, disappearing through a door at the back.

"Bleedin' hell Rayner, how did you manage to do that," the Superintendent muttered under his breath, his envious eyes tracking the exiting group.

The Commissioner had been too busy conversing with his own guests to see what had taken place, and when informed by

Morgan that the Inspector appeared to have abducted the star of the evening made an instant decision. He ordered the Head of his Detective Branch to go and find out what Rayner was up to, much to Morgan's delight.

After passing through the same door used to leave the reception by Rayner and those he had commandeered, Morgan found himself in yet another corridor. Nearby, a young man dressed in an evening suit stood looking extremely alert and circumspect outside a closed room. The guard had both hands grasped in front of him and turned his head in the Superintendent's direction, as Frederick Morgan approached. He was stopped in his tracks by the young man who explained a private meeting was ongoing inside the room, and that no unauthorised person was allowed entry.

Morgan produced his identity card and suggested the human obstacle stepped to one side or risked being arrested for obstructing the police.

"I am investigating a most serious crime of murder," Morgan stated, "Do I need to say anymore sunshine?"

The man immediately nodded his acquiescence but told the senior detective to wait whilst he announced the visitor's presence to those on the other side of the door. But the

Superintendent was too impatient for all of that kind of kerfuffle and spat out his protest.

"Get out of my bleedin' way," Morgan ordered, pushing the young man to one side, "I am a Scotland Yard detective investigating a murder, not some bleedin' immature fairy looking for an autograph."

After forcing his way into the room, the Superintendent was met by the sight of the small group of men and Clarice Rayner, sitting in armchairs in a semi-circle facing a blazing log fire. Upon seeing Morgan, Richard Rayner quickly got to his feet and introduced his senior officer to the others.

Morgan's aggressive attitude immediately vanished, only to be replaced by a figure of complete juvenile concession, who wasted little time in shaking the hand of his musical icon. This was the man he had worshipped from a far for so many years, holding Wagner in such high esteem and with such admiration he would often hum the tunes of some of the composer's favourite works whilst scrubbing himself down in his iron bath at home. Now, here he stood face to face with the genius from another Galaxy, in similar fashion to a besotted teenager falling in love for the first time.

"I have followed your works throughout most of my life sir," he embarrassingly stuttered, refusing to let go of the composer's hand, "And have been mesmerised by many of your works, including..."

"I beg you to stop Superintendent," Wagner ordered, raising the palm of his free hand, "Thank you for your charming acclamations, but time is short and I was about to answer the Inspector's question."

"What question was that?" Morgan enquired, his voice dropping down a decibel and looking directly at Richard Rayner after finally releasing the composer's professionally manicured hand.

"I have just described to Herr Wagner what has taken place upstairs and was asking if the name of Claude Grimbold meant anything to him."

"I'm afraid it doesn't Inspector," Wagner answered, in his usual pigeon English as he returned to his seat, "But I do accept your concerns that this awful incident could be related in some way to either myself or the concert performed tonight."

"It could also possibly be associated with the Royal Albert Hall itself," the manager, Bartholomew Franklin suggested with some anxiety.

"In what way sir?" Rayner asked, watching the Superintendent deliberately take a seat next to the composer.

"When Her Majesty commissioned the Hall to be built in honour of the late Prince Albert, there was a great deal of opposition regarding the cost and such like, and there were those who queried why the money hadn't been given to poor relief or to help the homeless of the city."

"And you suspect one or a number of those opponents could be responsible for the murder?" Rayner asked.

"It's the connection between the man who died and what you have told us, that he could be connected with a workhouse which leads me to such a suspicion Inspector."

"I think it's highly unlikely sir," Rayner admitted, "If that were to be the case, why murder a man when it might have been considered more newsworthy to set fire to the building or commit some severe damage. Why be instrumental in such a grievous felony on the night a Wagner concert was being performed?" The Inspector was already building a picture in his mind as to the possible motives behind the crime, or rather those intentions of the killer which failed to stand up. He was now anxious to return to the scene and hopefully be in a position to discuss the cause of death with the pathologist Doctor Critchley. Standing to his feet, he politely thanked those present for their time, Richard Wagner in particular.

After handing one of his cards to the composer, he confirmed, "I would be most appreciative should Claude Grimbold's name come to your attention in the future sir, or if you have some recollection of the man from the past, that I be informed as quickly as possible."

Wagner also rose from his seat and offered his hand to the Inspector.

"I shall give it careful consideration but as I have already said, at the moment the name means nothing to me."

Frederick Morgan couldn't stop bowing, as he and Clarice Rayner followed the Inspector from the room. Then he stopped and returned to where the composer was standing with his back to the fire and asked if Richard Wagner would sign his program.

"Of course Superintendent, what is your given name?"

"Frederick sir and thank you."

"A good German name," the famous man remarked, as he applied his signature to the programme offered.

No matter what the circumstances were surrounding that particular meeting, Frederick Morgan didn't care. He had met his musical hero in person and such a thrilling occasion would remain in his memory for the rest of his life.

Richard Rayner smiled and nodded at his wife in acknowledgement of the Superintendent's over-zealous joy, as all three then finally departed.

Chapter Four

Doctor Critchley was making his usual thorough cursory examination of the body when Richard Rayner arrived back in the smoking room, immediately attracting the pathologist's attention, which was sometimes difficult.

"There can be no doubt the victim died from a knife wound in the chest which has penetrated the heart," the specialist confirmed, "There is some bruising however visible on the face, but I shall know more once I have performed a post mortem back at the mortuary." The doctor then asked if the meat pie which was still resting on the table was connected in any way to the murder.

"At this moment in time doctor, the answer is that I honestly have no idea, but take it with the corpse just in case we discover that it is, although for the life of me I couldn't possibly guess why that should be."

The Inspector's principle concern was to discover the motive behind the killing, and Richard Rayner suspected that in this instance that might prove to be difficult. The fact the victim had been left to be discovered in such a high-profile location as the Royal Albert Hall, was not without purpose, or so he assumed. Also, the presence of the meat pie, if it was proved to be connected, could indicate that the killer possessed a complex mind, responsible for playing some bizarre game by introducing such a complication. But it was much too early yet to jump to any conclusions and he remained open minded on all possibilities.

The Inspector lifted the pastry from the table top, intending to pass it over to the doctor, when his eyes rested on something which confirmed the item was indeed, connected with the murder. There, stuck to the base of the pie was a small white label bearing the words, 'The first of many' crudely written across it.

"On second thoughts doctor, I think I should retain this back at Scotland Yard, as it does appear to be addressed to ourselves."

Arrangements were made to have the body removed to where the pathologist could continue his examination, and as far as

Rayner was concerned there was nothing more that could be done at the scene. Having made a point of wishing Henry and Nellie Bustle a goodnight, he and Clarice finally left the architectural landmark to head home.

On their journey, Clarice Rayner made a telling remark in the form of a question.

"Do you think the Pie-man will strike again Richard?"

"Your guess is as good as mine dear, but if he does, I do hope it's later rather than sooner as there is still plenty to do with this inquiry. I also believe you have just labelled the killer most appropriately by calling him the 'Pie-man'."

"Yes, it does seem to have a ring about it doesn't it, only I overheard Superintendent Morgan use the name when talking with the Commissioner earlier."

"Then it will most definitely be the epithet to describe the killer until he or she visits the hangman and perhaps even after that."

The following morning found the mortuary at St Mary's beckoning and Rayner was impatient to find out if the pathologist had uncovered any further information. During the carriage journey a mischievous Sergeant Bustle remarked on the Superintendent's behaviour that morning.

"I don't think he is in any fit state to assist us at present," he said, referring to the dazed condition Frederick Morgan appeared to be in, obviously the result of having personally met the famous composer a few hours earlier.

Rayner responded to the Sergeant's mischief by commenting that in his opinion the senior detective's absence wouldn't be missed, causing them to both chuckle at such an idea.

When they arrived at their destination, they found the elderly Doctor Albert Critchley hovering over the cadaver which had been received from the Royal Albert Hall earlier. For once he greeted the two detectives enthusiastically, which signalled to Richard Rayner the pathologist had made some interesting discoveries during his examination of Claude Grimbold's lifeless corpse.

"Your man died as a result of a single stab wound to the heart Inspector," he said, repeating his earlier findings back at the scene, "But notice the bruising around the eyes and across the ribs." Critchley was a man well into his sixties and certainly the most experienced pathologist in London at that time. His hardly visible white side whiskers matched the colour of his lengthy hair and he peered at both his visitors through a rimless pair of spectacles perched on the end of a pointed nose.

"It's quite obvious the man was subjected to a physical beating before being stabbed," Rayner acknowledged.

"Most definitely, but I do believe the physical attack would have taken place when the victim was not in a position to defend himself." The doctor then indicated burn marks on both wrists, before continuing, "These have been caused by pieces of rope or something similar, and indicate that at some time he was bound, most probably prior to being punched and kicked."

"Tortured then?"

The doctor nodded his agreement before clarifying, "Most certainly physically beaten."

"It seems highly unlikely that such activities would have taken place in a smoking room at the Royal Albert Hall, which means he was beaten about his face and body prior to being taken there. Is it possible the victim could have also been killed beforehand and then transported in some way to the same location he was found last night?"

"No," the doctor answered, "I believe he met his death there, where I examined him initially. I would estimate the time of death being around an hour before the victim was found, at approximately nine o'clock last night."

"When everyone present was seated in the auditorium

watching the Opera, including ourselves," Henry Bustle suggested.

"How long before his death do you think he was subjected to the physical attack doctor?" the Inspector asked.

"By the appearance of the bruising on the face and body, I would estimate the same day, certainly no later than six hours prior to him being stabbed. The colour of the bruising is still fairly intense with no signs of fading."

"So, what we have is a man who was physically attacked after having his wrists bound together, taken to the Royal Albert Hall and stabbed to death, having been forced to sit in a gentleman's smoking room. How on earth could he have been forced by the killer to go there dressed in an evening suit?"

"That would appear to be the case, but there is one other interesting feature which might answer your last query Inspector. There is the lingering odour of opium-based laudanum around his mouth, which I believe had been administered in a large amount, probably sufficient to create drowsiness but falling just short of orchestrating his death. It would certainly result in his compliance by being unaware of what he was doing."

Rayner turned to Henry Bustle and stated the obvious assumption, as if the Sergeant was deaf or lacking the ability to comprehend, "That would have been used to assist in getting the victim into the Royal Albert Hall without him being capable of resistance."

Bustle nodded his understanding, puzzled as to why he should not have already known that from what the doctor had told them. It was unlike Richard Rayner to cause him such embarrassment and assumed the Inspector's mind was focusing perhaps too much on the salient points being made by the pathologist.

After thanking the doctor for his assistance, the two detectives left and once outside, Rayner referred to the handwritten note found on the base of the meat pie.

"If that short message was indeed written by the killer Henry, then it can only mean we can expect more victims slain by the same hand in the near future."

"Or, might it just be our man's bizarre way of bragging about what he had achieved?"

"Possibly, but we still need to act with some urgency, just in case others have been lined up in some kind of ritualistic or revengeful chain."

"Where to next Inspector?" the Sergeant enquired, as their carriage was driven out through the main hospital gates.

"I think it's time for us to visit the Upper Clapton Workhouse in Pond Lane, to see what information they can give us regarding our Mr. Claude Grimbold."

Henry Bustle gave a forlorn shrug and admitted, "That's one visit I'm not looking forward to sir."

The workhouse was situated in a rural area of London, and was comprised of a dismal looking large farmhouse which had been converted and was fronted by a long drive leading off Pond Lane in Upper Clapton. There was no warm welcome to greet the detectives and the reception area was small, cold and dark, with just two oil lamps burning on a far wall. An elderly grey-haired gentleman was sitting behind a table looking far less heathy than the corpse they had just left.

"I wonder if the rest of the building is as dismal as this," Bustle whispered, staring across at the ghost like figure appearing to fit in well with the cold depressing blandness of the reception area, "It gives me the creeps, imagine having to live and work here and with that wondering around the corridors," he said, referring to the aged receptionist.

After Richard Rayner had introduced them to the old man and requested to speak to someone in charge, the receptionist just nodded and disappeared through a door on the far side.

Whilst kept waiting, Henry Bustle perused a number of painted portraits hanging from the surrounding walls, all purporting to be former governors and managers of the unsavoury establishment. After stopping at one particular profile, he called the Inspector over to him.

"Can you see the name beneath the portrait?"

"Claude Grimbold."

The two detectives glanced at each other, just as the door opened and an elderly, fragile woman entered the reception area, grasping both hands in front of her. She looked overworked and under fed as she introduced herself as being, Gladys Grimbold, the Mistress of the Workhouse.

Again, the two visitors looked at each other in recognition of the name presented, and Rayner asked if he was correct in believing that Mr. Claude Grimbold was the Master of the Workhouse and husband of the lady they were standing face to face with.

"Yes Inspector," she confirmed, "But I'm afraid he's missing at present, that is to say he left here on business yesterday morning and has not yet returned."

"Is there somewhere private we can go to Mrs. Grimbold?" Rayner enquired.

She nodded and still grasping her hands nervously, requested they followed her.

After leaving the front of the building, the detectives were escorted down a dark corridor until they reached a small office at the far end. There was a lot more natural light entering the room through a pair of French windows, and the lady sat behind an old desk from which the varnish had disappeared a long time before. She invited her visitors to take advantage of two armchairs.

"Now sir, how can I help you?" she asked, raising her chin and looking devotedly ascetic.

For all the woman's aura of superiority, Rayner was concerned that she didn't look to be in the best of health and wondered whether the news he was about to share with her, might be too much for the Mistress to handle. However, having established she was the wife of the murdered victim, she had to be told of the fate of her husband.

"I'm afraid I have some very bad news Mrs. Grimbold concerning your husband."

They both saw the woman make a distinct effort to straighten her back and steel herself in readiness.

"I am so sorry to have to tell you this, but I'm afraid he's dead."

At first, she didn't say a word and just sat there staring back at the Inspector with expressionless eyes. Then, as if suddenly recognising the devastating nature of his words, she quietly croaked, "What do you mean he's dead? That is impossible."

"I'm afraid he was found murdered at the Royal Albert Hall last night," Rayner confirmed, trying to be as sensitive as he possibly could.

Still the woman's face offered nothing, as if her dyed in the wool features were set in concrete.

"We can call back if you wish."

She then asked, showing no sign of emotion, "How was he murdered Inspector?"

"He was stabbed through the heart madam." Rayner was reluctant to mention the fact that her husband had also been subjected to a physical beating. That would come later.

"Have you any idea who might have wanted your husband dead?"

"No, I have none but I take it you have not yet caught the murderer?"

"Not yet, but we shall find your husband's killer I can assure you. Can you tell us on what kind of business he went on yesterday morning and what time he left here?"

"On business connected with the establishment," she snapped back, "And he left in the trap at about eight o'clock yesterday morning. Do you know what he was doing at the Royal Albert Hall?"

"We were hoping you might be able to tell us that Mrs. Grimbold."

She shook her head before declaring, "I have no idea."

Rayner needed to find out more about the kind of business in which the murdered victim was intending to settle, but thought that particular time was inappropriate to delve too deeply into their affairs. It was strange however, that she had not yet showed any signs of outward grief or any other kind of affection.

Then both detectives overheard a faint noise coming from the other side of the closed door, and whilst Richard Rayner continued to question the Mistress about matters concerning the workhouse, Henry Bustle silently stepped across the room, before placing a hand on the handle of the door. When, without warning, he yanked it open, there standing with a vase full of fresh flowers was a small, slim lady with dark hair showing signs of silver streaks. It was obvious she had been taken unaware by the Sergeant and immediately entered the room, before placing the vase on top of the desk.

"I'm sorry to interrupt Mrs. Grimbold," she quietly said, but with a hint of agitation in her voice, "I wasn't aware you had visitors."

"That's alright, Nellie," the Mistress replied, before waiting for the employee to leave the room. Once she had left, the woman in charge explained, "Nellie Pritchard is our Housekeeper and likes to keep abreast of events," she said, referring to the obvious fact that the female visitor to the office had been undoubtedly ear wigging at the door.

Rayner just nodded, before standing to leave and thanking the woman for her time. In a strange way he felt that he and Henry Bustle had been intruding on something he couldn't quite recognise at that moment; some kind of mystery Gladys Grimbold was reluctant to discuss.

"We shall call again," he confirmed, "At a better time, when you have been given an opportunity to come to terms with your husband's passing."

Again, there was no acknowledgement and the Mistress just sat there staring back at him without saying a word.

Rayner had the impression the woman was more concerned with having received a visit from two Scotland Yard detectives, rather than having just received notice of her husband's brutal murder. It was something which would be worthwhile pursuing, but much later.

As their carriage pulled away from the front of the house, Henry Bustle had a few remarks he wished to make.

"I don't think that woman is human," he admitted, "Either that or we should regard her as a principle suspect behind her husband's death."

"People have different ways of grieving, Henry. We must be patient and leave it a few days before returning. We need to know where Claude Grimbold was heading when he left there yesterday morning, and what the nature of his business was."

"It seemed to me she had no intention of telling us Inspector."

Rayner smiled and explained, "It's early days yet, we shall have our information eventually."

When they returned to Scotland Yard, they found the Superintendent sitting in Rayner's chair, holding a glass of malt whiskey in one hand and the signed programme from the previous night in the other.

"My God Rayner," he said, in a way of greeting the two detectives back to the fold, "I still cannot believe I shook the hand of the great Wagner."

"Did he offer you a partnership in his theatre in Germany sir,"

Henry Bustle jocularly enquired.

"If you've nothing constructive to say, Bustle, then keep your mouth shut."

"Yes sir."

Morgan then enquired with Richard Rayner whether there had been any progress thus far, and the Inspector briefly discussed the inscription found on the meat pie.

"What do you deduce from the handwriting?" Morgan asked.

"It appears to have been made by an uneducated hand and yet there are no spelling mistakes. I suspect the writer intended to disguise it." He then went on to describe the pathologist's findings, before giving a brief summary of their meeting at the workhouse.

"They should set fire to every one of those depressing social mishaps,"
Morgan said, vacating Rayner's chair and sitting on one of the other more basic wooden seats.

"I appreciate they never seem to appear more than just impoverished institutions sir," the Inspector answered, "But they do save lives, especially those who are found starving and with nowhere to live."

"Have we uncovered a motive for the murder yet?"

"No sir, but even at this early stage of the Inquiry I find myself leaning towards the victim's place of employment being connected in some way."

"What kind of a place is it? If it's anything like the workhouses I've visited in the past I suspect it's pretty gruesome."

"Oh yes sir, it's certainly not failing in that respect."

"Neither is the lady who runs the place," Henry Bustle added.

Chapter Five

Although lacking in style or panache, Henry Bustle's usually drab dress code could most certainly be described as being extremely practical and hard wearing. Having a wife and four kids to support, the Sergeant could not afford to be as extravagant as his Inspector and his change of attire was far less frequent, the same jacket and trousers being subjected to quite rigorous wear and tear on a daily basis. Also, with a face resembling a street affray divided by a scar running down one side of it, he resembled a bare-knuckled fighter rather than a detective employed by the Metropolitan Police. And yet that kind of functional and practical outlook had been the magnetic attraction which had earned the man the utmost respect and dependability from Richard Rayner. Henry Bustle was not only reliable but in the Inspector's eyes, completely trustworthy – a major and rare characteristic asset.

As he paced his way through the front reception area of Scotland Yard, the Sergeant's attention was drawn to what appeared to be an ongoing ruckus between the desk sergeant and a member of the public. Bustle stopped and continued to observe the incident with some interest.

The complainant appeared to be a vociferous coal merchant; a strong looking man wearing a leather head covering and apron, and whose face was just turning from red to purple beneath a covering of coal dust. Upon enquiring what all the hullaballoo was about, the detective was quickly enlightened by the desk sergeant, who seemed relieved at the sight of an ally who might be willing to enter the fracas in his support.

"This is Mr. Porter from George Street, Henry, just south of the river," the official in charge of the front desk explained, "He had two brays taken during the night."

"Stolen they was from right under my nose. It's them Irish bastards who's done it," the complainant alleged.

"Settle down Mr. Porter ..."

"Settle down? I'm finished do you hear me; finished without them two horses to pull the carts." Porter then turned to the man whom he had been arguing and pointedly asked, jerking a thumb in the new-comers direction, "Who is this geezer anyway?"

"This is Sergeant Bustle from the Detective Branch who might be able to help you, if you listen to him."

"He looks more like one of them mountebank's who's nicked my two brays."

"I understand how you must feel at the moment Mr. Porter, but taking the piss out of me isn't going to get them back."

The desk sergeant nodded at the complaining man who immediately attempted some kind of mumbled apology without actually succeeding.

"The problem is I've got twelve loads to deliver on the cart as I speak, with no bloody horses to pull it."

Sergeant Claude Davey from the same department in which Henry Bustle worked, unexpectedly appeared on the scene. He was a tall, bald-headed man with considerable experience in crime investigation and suggested to Bustle that he could look into the alleged crime, an offer welcomed by Richard Rayner's right-hand man.

The aggrieved coal merchant was then taken away by Davey to discuss the matter further and in a more private environment. At least what followed was the restoration of a more peaceful environment to the reception area. When both the detective and complainant had disappeared from sight, Henry Bustle turned to the previously besieged Sergeant and enquired, "Have we had any other reports of horses being stolen, Reg?"

"As a matter of fact we have. Hang on a minute."

The Sergeant then produced a large book from under the counter and began to thumb through the pages. He explained, "Over the past month or so there's been three reports of horses being stolen, all it seems, having been taken during the night."

"Can you get the constables who initially dealt with each of those larcenies to submit full detailed reports to me personally Reg. I think this might be worth looking into, especially if there's a pattern."

"There's a lot of people who'd be thankful for that Henry. I suspect those, like Mr. Porter there who use their nags for commercial reasons, would have been put out of business."

"That's exactly why I'd like to know more about what's been going on mate."

Most of Clarice Rayners time spent at Kings College was undergoing various research projects into her chosen subject, which was facial-reconstruction. She frequently corresponded with Professor Hermann Welcker at the University of Giessen who had originally pioneered the subject, and between the two academics a great deal of progress had been achieved. As part of her conditions of employment at the college, Clarice was also required to deliver the occasional lecture and on this particular morning, the lecture hall was filled to capacity. When she entered the seat of learning, all seventy plus students gave her their attention, enthusiastically anticipating a most informative input by the lady researcher.

Standing at a lectern on a raised stage and facing her audience, Clarice Rayner pointed to a number of items sitting on top of a table behind where she stood.

Speaking clearly, she said, "The first item you can see is a replica of a skull found buried in a hedgerow adjacent to St Dunstan's Church in Spitalfields. I had been requested by Scotland Yard to attempt to re-create the face which once belonged to the victim, and the result was the bust you can see next to the skull."

"Was it your husband Miss who asked you to do that?" a student sitting on the front row boldly asked, "We all know he's a famous detective."

Brushing aside the brash inference, Clarice answered back, "Master Grimes, that has nothing to do with the subject we are studying this morning," before continuing with her lecture.

"The victim was eventually identified as having been a young lady from Wolverhampton, which assisted the police in finally securing the conviction of a man for the woman's murder."

The same student who had just interrupted the flow of the lecture raised his hand, but was ignored by Clarice who preferred to describe the manner in which the result of the project was proven to be accurate.

"The victim's sister had attended the mortuary at St Mary's Hospital where the facial reconstruction had taken place, and by looking directly at the finished item, immediately identified her unfortunate sibling."

Young Grimes's hand was still wavering in the air, so the female lecturer finally capitulated and gave him the floor.

"Is it possible to reconstruct the face of a horse miss?" he asked, seemingly genuinely interested.

"Yes, I believe so," Clarice answered, to a background of juvenile sniggering, "But I cannot think of any circumstances when such a requirement would be necessary."

"What if the horse was a famous and very expensive race horse stolen one night from its stable, after the guard had been drugged?"

For a moment, Clarice just looked at the student, suspecting he was referring to a real-life incident.

"Are you personally aware of such circumstances Master Grimes?" she asked.

"Yes miss, only last night my father's favourite horse, Fleet of Foot, was stolen and they found the lad employed to keep a vigilance drugged up to his eyeballs. The horse was a favourite to win this year's Derby at Epsom Miss, and my father is beside himself." Such a declaration certainly added some spice to the lady's lecture and a discussion followed revolving around the possibility of reconstruction being applied to the skulls of animals, in particular, horses.

Richard Rayner felt a need to revisit the scene of Claude Grimbold's murder at the Royal Albert Hall. There were a number of unanswered questions which needed addressing, such as, how the victim got there in the first place? Was there any other means of entering the building, avoiding the main entrance? Also, the Inspector had failed to come to terms with the fact the murder had taken place during a concert given by Wagner. He felt there was some significance involved, and hoped that by learning more of the circumstances in which the murder had been committed, a possible motive might come to light.

As he was about to take possession of his top coat and hat, the desk sergeant appeared in the doorway to his office and informed Rayner there was a lady downstairs in the reception, enquiring if she could speak to him or Sergeant Bustle.

"Very well Reg," the Inspector confirmed, "She can speak to both of us." He then asked his own Sergeant to show the lady visitor up to his office, before returning to the seat behind his desk.

Rayner was surprised when Henry Bustle returned and showed the lady into the office. It was Nellie Pritchard, the House Keeper from the Upper Clapton Workhouse.

After offering the lady a seat, the Inspector took a moment to study his visitor. She was a frail middle-aged lady, who by her appearance was probably paid just sufficient in wages to survive. He noticed how worn her laced up boots were and saw visible signs of mud had been splashed on to the bottom of her ankle length coat. Upon enquiring as to how she had journeyed to Scotland Yard the lady told him.

"I've walked sir," she meekly answered.

"All the way from Upper Clapton?"

She nodded, almost ashamedly and Rayner guessed she was a

woman with principles, the kind who would never seek either charity or pity. He also made a mental note of her mature attractiveness, deciding that the lady would have been even more attractive in her younger years.

After asking Henry Bustle to fetch some tea, he then enquired, "How then can I be of help to you Miss Pritchard. I take it you are not married?"

"No sir, I was never blessed with that opportunity," she confessed, sitting upright with a claret felt hat perched on top of her head, decorated by a small feather on one side. The colour of the hat matched the coat she was wearing, with fur trimmings on the collar and sleeves, an item of clothing clearly having been cleaned and ironed many times previously. It was quite obvious that Miss Pritchard had donned on her Sunday best for the occasion.

Rayner just nodded, and sat back waiting for his visitor to converse further.

"I'm not sure if I am doing the right thing coming to see you like this Mr. Rayner," she said, apologetically, "I feel that in some way, I am being disloyal."

"Let me be the judge of that dear lady."

"Well, it's about the Master, Mr. Grimbold, and I suppose his wife who is my employer."

"Please go on."

"I've never been one to gossip and heaven forbid, I have never told tales out of school. I am a religious woman sir and believe in practising my Christian beliefs whenever possible."

"I have no doubt of that Miss Pritchard."

"I have to go back twenty years or so when we had one child in particular staying with us. He was an innocent eight-year old boy by the name of Thomas Wake, whose mother had recently died at a young age. Poor Tommy was left alone to fend for himself at the workhouse. Sadly, he seemed to aggravate both Mr. and Mrs. Grimbold, not intentionally mind you, but it was as though every time he erred in some way, no matter how small or insignificant, he was subjected to the most cruel and wicked retribution, so severe it seemed to be unnatural."

"In what way?" Rayner asked.

"The boy seemed to spend more time in the coal cellar than he did in his own bed in the dormitory with the other children. If for example, he just accidentally spilt a drink, down to the coal cellar he would go and remain there sometimes for nights and days. If he was slow in understanding what was being said to him, the same course of action would be taken. In between events such as those, he was also frequently birched for incidents which other children would have been chastised and nothing more. I still shudder at the memory of the scars left on his back and buttocks."

Henry Bustle then entered the room with a tray of cups and pot of tea, which their visitor was extremely thankful for.

Rayner also stretched to reach into a set of drawers at the side of his desk and produced a small tin of biscuits before handing it to Mrs. Pritchard.

"Please be our guest and have as many as you wish," he offered.

"Thank you, sir."

"So, for the Sergeant's benefit, this eight-year old boy, Thomas Wake, was in your opinion subjected to extensive and unnecessary cruelty by both Mr. and Mrs. Grimbold some twenty years ago and for the most insignificant misdemeanours. What eventually happened to the boy?"

"He left the workhouse and was transferred to another, I believe in Lambeth and I never set eyes on him since the day he was taken through the front door for the last time." She paused to cast her mind back further and then remarked on the way in which the same boy would be left in the freezing cold conditions of the rat-infested cellar, without food or drink for sometimes up to three or four days and nights.

"I used to creep down there and provide him with some scraps I could get from the kitchen and bottles of water, but it was difficult as Mrs. Grimbold was constantly watchful."

"And I assume by coming and telling us this, you suspect that Thomas Wake, who would now be a fully grown twenty-eight-year-old man, could possibly have sought his revenge on the Master of the workhouse by killing him?"

"That is not the main reason for my visiting you sir," Nellie Pritchard confessed, after taking a drink from her tea cup, "God punishes those who have sinned and I have come here to ensure that the cruel and wicked way in which that boy was treated is made known. If Tommy Wake's hand was responsible for the murder of Claude Grimbold, then his wife was as much to blame sir by condoning and on occasions encouraging, such wickedness and cruelty."

"Have you any idea where Master Wake is now? Perhaps in London or further afield?"

"No sir, I only remember he had a younger sister who was kept in the workhouse in Lambeth, that being the reason for Tommy being moved there so both siblings could be closer to each other."

"It sounds as though such a move was a blessing," Henry Bustle remarked.

Rayner sat back once again, and allowed a short period for the lady visitor to devour a few biscuits from the tin. He then rose from his seat and thanked her for her attendance.

"The Sergeant will arrange some transport for you to return to Upper Clapton Miss Pritchard."

"I only ask Inspector that our conversation remains confidential and I wouldn't wish for anyone where I work to know I've come here today. I can only hope I have done the right thing."

"I can assure you dear lady, what you have told us will be of great help." Rayner knew only too well that without people with the same courage as Nellie Pritchard the job of the police would be far more difficult.

"Have no fear, the Sergeant will drop you off well away from your place of employment and I guarantee you nothing about our discussion will be mentioned outside this room."

She visibly relaxed and smiled for the first time, before disappearing through the door in the company of the caring Henry Bustle.

Chapter Six

The empty auditorium seemed strangely enigmatically and awesomely void following the tumultuous assembly occupying the seats the last time they visited the Royal Albert Hall. The two detectives stood for a moment looking up at the surrounding interior and balconies, admiring what appeared to Richard Rayner to resemble a decorated multi-tiered Christmas cake. A few cleaners could be seen working with feather dusters, buckets and mops, as they manoeuvred their way down the various aisles, weaving in and out of the numerous rows of seats. The Grand Wagner Festival was still top of the bill and a few of the singers were present on the stage, quietly rehearsing. Then a small man, dressed in just an open necked shirt and waistcoat joined them, enquiring if he could be of any assistance.

It was Henry Bustle who introduced the Scotland Yard detectives.

"Ah I see," the man acknowledged, "Then gentlemen you will

need to see Mr. Bartholomew Franklin, the manager. I shall fetch him for you."

"Thank you," Rayner said, "But could you ask Mr. Franklin to join us at the gentlemen's smoking room where the crime took place the other evening."

The man nodded and quickly disappeared.

When they reached the location in which Claude Grimbold had been found, it was in complete darkness. The light that came from the windows situated in the outside corridor did not reach beyond the door.

"From the smell of disinfectant sir, I assume everything inside here has been cleaned."

"As we would expect Henry, but I'm not particularly interested in the room's interior, but the route the killer took and the method he used to get his victim here in the first place. From what the young waitress Mary Marchant told us, there was no one left inside the room following the intermission."

"That was confirmed by a number of the other members of staff who made statements sir," Bustle added.

"Which means the killer brought his victim here during the second half of the concert, obviously unseen. But how? We know that Master Grimbold was drugged at the time so I suspect the man wouldn't have known much about what he was doing or to where he was walking."

Bartholomew Franklin was wearing casual clothing, in contrast to his more formal attire when Rayner had previously made his acquaintance in the presence of Richard Wagner. He was a most amicable middle-aged gentleman and when he spoke, the Inspector detected a slight foreign accent which he hadn't previously noticed. When asked about it, the concert hall manager smiled and confessed he had been raised in Paris by his mother who had been a French lady married to an English gentleman.

"After being brought to England at a very early age, English soon became my first language," he explained, "Although I also learned to speak German over a period of time spent in Bayreuth."

"Richard Wagner's theatre?" Rayner asked.

"Yes, the Bayreuth Festspeilhaus where I was the manager there before accepting my current position at this magnificent Royal Albert Hall."

"Now I see how you managed to secure Wagner's attendance here."

Bartholomew Franklin gave a short bow of his head and then

enquired as to how he could be of further assistance to the detectives.

"I assume there are other entrances into the Hall Mr. Franklin, apart from the main entrance," the Inspector said.

"Yes, there are a number of side entrances around the perimeter of the building."

"Are they all kept locked during a performance?"

"No, once a performance begins, they are unlocked and remain so until the audience have left at the end of the evening's entertainment, in case of fire or some other mishap in which we have to evacuate the building as a matter of urgency."

"Excellent, then pray tell me which is the entrance closest to where we are now standing?"

"Come gentlemen, I will show you." The manager then led his two visitors for a short way along the corridor before turning into an alcove in which there were two swinging doors leading to a staircase. They followed their escort down two flights until reaching a pair of double doors opening out onto the street.

"During the second half of the concert, am I right in assuming this entrance would be unattended?" Rayner asked.

"Yes, you are Inspector. Once the concert has started stewards attend and unlock each of the side doors. They return once the building has been vacated and the doors are again secured."

"Who would be aware of such practice, Mr. Franklin?"

"Just about every member of staff and of course, anybody who has been employed by the Royal Albert Hall in the past."

"Thank you, sir, you have been most helpful"

Richard Rayner now knew the route the killer had taken before and after committing the murder.

"The only downside to that sir, is that the man we seek obviously gained access into the building without the need to purchase tickets," Henry Bustle suggested, as they sat opposite each other in the enclosed carriage returning them to Scotland Yard.

"Yes Henry, that does cancel out another line of inquiry I was hoping might have been useful to us."

The Sergeant then mentioned the recent and unusual spate of larcenies involving the stealing of horses and wondered if it was possible, he could make some enquiries of his own. But his Inspector was reluctant to concede to his request.

"Albeit I am aware of your love for those four-legged animals Henry, I do believe this murder must take precedence over everything else, for now in any case."

"Of course, sir."

When they arrived at Scotland Yard, they found Superintendent Morgan waiting in the front reception. He looked extremely anxious and upon seeing his two detectives appear, immediately went across to them loudly declaring, "God Almighty Rayner, where the bloody hell have you been? There's been another one."

The Royal Strand Theatre in Westminster was popular for the number of operettas it supported and once again, Frederick Morgan was keen to become involved with his favourite past time. However, he was only there as an investigator accompanying Richard Rayner and Henry Bustle, and not as a paying or invited customer to watch a show.

The three detectives were met in the main reception area by the theatre manager, Alfred Snipe, a tall distinguished man with grey hair parted down the centre, who was as immaculately dressed as Richard Rayner.

After the initial introductions, the manager led the investigators into the auditorium which was a lot smaller than the Royal Albert Hall and certainly less grandiose, but still retaining an impressive interior. Two constables had already been dispatched to the premises and were found standing in an aisle leading from the back of the spacious room, near the front of the stage. To their right, slouched back in an aisle seat, was the figure of a man who Rayner calculated would have been in his early fifties. He was a tall, spindly built individual dressed in dark clothing, with fair bushy hair going grey and mutton chop whiskers. There was no doubt the victim had expired and the front of his vest, visible from beneath a jacket, was saturated in blood. But the most unusual aspect of the man's posture was the manner in which he sat with his head bowed, as if asleep. But what caught the detectives' immediate attention was the sight of a crusty pie resting in his lap, seemingly untouched.

"Well gents, it appears that our killer has a sense of humour," Morgan remarked, referring to the presence of the pastry and grasping the pie to look at the base. Sure enough, a small white label was attached to the bottom with the words, 'Revenge is mine sayeth the Lord'.

"Christ Rayner, he'll be sending us bleedin' telegrams next," Morgan quipped.

"It does appear that he remains intent on leaving us acknowledgements with his victims."

"But why, what does he get out of doing that?" Henry Bustle asked.

"That's for us to find out Henry," Rayner suggested, "Perhaps he will enlighten us once we come face to face with him."

The anxious theatre manager explained that the body was found that morning when the cleaners first arrived at the theatre.

"And you are absolutely certain it wasn't here last night following the performance?"

"I am absolutely sure," Alfred Snipe confirmed, "I personally check all the rows of seats and lavatories before finally closing the building and locking up."

"Have we any idea at all how this corpse managed to find this seat, obviously during the night. I take it there is no sign of any forced entry?"

"None whatsoever; it was the first thing I checked after the body had been discovered."

"What performance did you put on last night Mr. Snipe?" Morgan asked.

"Madame Favart, an operetta by Jacques Offenbach. The French composer is touring this country at present."

"And how big was the audience last night sir?" Rayner enquired.

"We had a full house; a complete sell out."

"I've sent for the doctor who should be here soon," Morgan

confirmed, as Rayner leant forward to begin searching through the pockets of the dead man's jacket. He found a card with the name and address of one Elias Thompson printed thereon from the Christchurch Workhouse in Newgate Street.

"Bleedin' hell Rayner, why doesn't that surprise me?"

When Doctor Albert Critchley arrived, he soon confirmed the victim had been stabbed in the chest and with Frederick Morgan's permission, suggested the dead man be removed to the mortuary as quickly as possible for further examination.

"Wait doctor," the Inspector insisted, "Can you tell us whether the man was killed here, or his lifeless body brought into the theatre post death?"

"From the amount of blood present, I would guess that he was stabbed where he is now seated, but I would need to test that theory back at the mortuary."

Rayner nodded his understanding and turning to the theatre manager asked if the lights in the auditorium could be turned up fully, but was informed they were already in that position. The Inspector slowly walked up the aisle towards the back of the room, carefully studying the strip of carpet which ran down the length from the front of the stage to the back of the auditorium.

When he returned to the small group, he told the pathologist,

"Very well doctor, nothing more can be gained from delaying the dead man's removal."

"What's your opinion Rayner on these bloody pies and cryptic messages stuck to them?" the Superintendent asked.

"My initial thoughts are that our killer has a twisted belief that what he is doing is justifiable and in his bizarre way, he is trying to tell us just that. His last message tends to add support to my own suspicion that the motive is one of revenge."

"In other words, he's some kind of cranky bastard."

"Not necessarily Superintendent, there appears to be purpose behind leaving an untouched pie after each of his two murders, and I fear there is the existence of some sinister intention behind such an act."

"Don't tell me he's intending to poison all the bakers in London?"

"He is working to an agenda," Rayner suggested, ignoring Morgan's jibe, "A list of individuals I believe he intends to kill for whatever reason, and the purpose for leaving a meat pie behind is his way of receiving recognition for his work, and as I have suggested already, communicating to us some bizarre justification for his actions." Rayner then looked directly into Morgan's eyes and proclaimed, "If I am correct in my assumption, the man is extremely likely to strike again."

"Unless we catch him first."

"Obviously, but I shall be interested to learn more about Mr. Elias Thompson's background. That will be our starting point from which we shall investigate this second murder."

"I had no idea we had started the investigation into the first one Rayner," the Superintendent remarked with some sarcasm, and pulling up his trousers as they were beginning to slip down from his waistline, having forgotten to wear his bracers earlier.

"Oh, I think we have progressed considerably with our investigation into Claude Grimbold. For instance, we are now aware it appears he was a cruel man who as a result of his past activities might well have attracted a number of people who would wish him dead. However, the death of the unfortunate Elias Thompson places more emphasis on both murders being linked by the influence of work houses. There is now much to do and I wish to make a suggestion to you if I may."

Following a request from Richard Rayner for the secondment of Sergeant Jack Robinson to his team of investigators, Frederick Morgan acted quickly and within a couple of hours the young officer who had assisted both Rayner and Bustle on many previous Inquiries, made himself available in the Inspector's office at Scotland Yard. After updating the new addition on the events which had taken place over the past week or so, Rayner then turned to Henry Bustle and suggested he try and find out as much as possible about the history of Thomas Wake, the boy mentioned by Nellie Pritchard.

"The lady told us that she thought he'd been transferred to a workhouse in Lambeth Henry, so that might be the best place to begin."

"Yes sir."

"Jack, I want you to visit the Christchurch Workhouse in Newgate Street and find out as much as you can about our second victim, Elias Thompson. What position, if any, did he hold there and for how long? Has there ever been an individual likely to hold some kind of grudge against the man? But tread warily, you will first need to find out if the victim had any relatives connected with the same establishment who would not yet be aware of his demise."

"I'll leave immediately Inspector."

"And Jack," Rayner said with a smile, "Welcome back."

"Thank you, sir."

"Might I ask what you will be doing Inspector?" Henry Bustle enquired.

"I intend to revisit the Upper Clapton Workhouse and obtain more precise information as to the kind of business which attracted Claude Grimbold away on the day he was murdered."

When Richard Rayner stepped down from his carriage outside the front door of the workhouse, people could have been forgiven for mistaking him for a Vaudeville entertainer, from his dashing style of attire. His taste for vivid bright colours would often make other men cringe, in particular Frederick Morgan, but Rayner was his own man, uninfluenced by the thoughts of others. When he married Clarice there were many who hoped he would be persuaded to wear less flamboyant attire, but alas, such hopes never came to fruition.

After entering the Institution, the cheerfully clad Inspector was surprised to see Nellie Pritchard standing in the small reception area talking with the old man who had met them on their previous visit.

"Good afternoon madam," he politely announced, not wanting to show any closer relationship with the House Keeper than one previous casual meeting.

"Good afternoon Inspector," she quietly answered, "Have you

come to see the Mistress?"

"That I have, is she available please?"

"I'm afraid not sir. She is so distraught following the news of her husband I'm afraid Mrs. Grimbold has taken to her bed."

"Then perhaps you can help me Mrs. Pritchard, I just have one or two questions I need to ask."

"Of course Inspector, I shall do my best; please follow me."

The lady led the way to the same office in which Rayner and Bustle had engaged the Mistress on their earlier visit.

"How can I assist sir?" the House Keeper enquired, standing in the centre of the room, as if she wanted to avoid touching anything habitually used by Mrs. Grimbold.

"When we called previously, your employer informed us that her husband had left at eight o'clock that morning to attend to some business. Unfortunately, I was of the impression she was in no real state of mind to be probed further, and I am now wondering if you have any idea of the kind of business trip Mr. Grimbold undertook on that day?"

"The Master never discussed his business affairs with any of us Inspector, and there was certainly no mention of where he intended to go on that occasion."

"Then tell me, what kind of business transactions would the

Master of a workhouse be likely to become involved in?"

"I should imagine various negotiations connected with suppliers and the such like for the House." She lowered her voice to almost a whisper when continuing, "But I am aware that Mr. Grimbold had a passion for the turf, if that's of any help to you."

"You mean horse racing?"

The lady silently nodded.

"Was he a betting man then?"

"I'm not sure, but it did seem likely. I often heard him mention locations such as Newmarket and Epsom and on one occasion recently, I found him studying a form chart which listed the horses selected to run in the Derby, but again I'm only telling you this in the strictest of confidence."

"Of course, you have been a great help Miss Pritchard, thank you."

Chapter Seven

"Do you know what Rayner?" Frederick Morgan said, speaking through a smoke screen which was becoming more denser each time he sucked on his pipe, "I think our killer could be a baker."

"Because of the meat pies he leaves at each of his murders?"

"I think he's taunting us by deliberately leaving us with a clue as to his identity. Have one of your men make enquiries with those who supplied bread to each of the workhouses."

"But what of a motive sir?" Rayner asked, "Why should a baker murder two of his customers?"

Morgan shrugged his shoulders before suggesting, "They might have failed to pay their bills and accumulated so much debt they could never be in a position to pay it off. I think it's worthy of consideration."

The Inspector thought the idea was preposterous, but didn't

wish to rock the pipe smoker's boat. He did however put forward his own theory.

"I suspect the reason behind the killings is much deeper than that and from what we have gleaned thus far, is sourced from an overwhelming desire for revenge sir."

"I agree. Revenge for not paying their bills."

"We shall see sir."

As if on cue, young Jack Robinson appeared in the open doorway of the Superintendent's office and was immediately told to enter. The Sergeant looked optimistic and briefly shared with the two senior detectives the intelligence he'd obtained relating to the second victim, Elias Thompson.

"Up until a month ago, Thompson was the Master of the Christchurch Workhouse, before retiring to allegedly live in the country."

"Do we know whereabouts, Jack?" Rayner quickly asked.

"No sir. According to a Mrs Entwhistle the House Keeper there, he never actually moved out of his room at the House. Apparently, his possession of the property he was purchasing and in which he intended to spend his retirement was delayed, and he remained where he had worked for the past twenty years. It was just a matter of time before Thompson would eventually leave."

"Is there a Mrs. Thompson?" Morgan asked.

"No sir. There used to be but she passed on a few years ago and our man never remarried, throwing himself into his work at the Institution."

"What else did you find out about him?" Rayner then enquired.

"He was well respected by his staff and they all showed both shock and horror when I told them of his unfortunate ending. Again, according to Alice Entwhistle, he was perhaps a little over enthusiastic with the birch when dealing with young miscreants, but as she said herself, a good thrashing never hurt any boy."

"So, he displayed characteristics of cruelty, is that it Jack?"

"No sir, cruelty appears to be the wrong descriptive word. From what I was told I got the impression that he was over enthusiastic but not exactly cruel towards the children in his care."

"Did she or any of the other members of staff know of anyone, man or boy, who might have borne a grudge against the Master?"

"No sir, my general view was that Elias Thompson was a fairly popular man and an excellent people motivator, and those I spoke with enjoyed working for him."

"Did the man have any interests outside the workhouse Jack?"

"Apparently, he was a regular attendant at the theatre sir, and would go to see whichever took his fancy at least once a week."

"In between placing wagers at the track." the Superintendent suggested.

"Strangely you should say that sir, because apparently he also enjoyed visiting race track meetings whenever he had the opportunity, a habit which the others condemned, not feeling it was befitting of the Master of a Christian workhouse."

"Well, I shan't be applying for his job in that case," Morgan quipped, "What next Rayner?"

The Inspector turned to Jack Robinson and suggested, "You can come with me now Jack to see what the pathologist has for us, but that is an unusual coincidence."

"What is?" the Superintendent asked.

"Both of our victims had a preference for the turf."

They found Doctor Critchley sitting in his office busy writing up his report on the latest post mortem. He welcomed Rayner and Robinson, before explaining, "There are many similarities between both of your victims Inspector. As with the first, Elias Thompson died as a result of a stab wound to his heart, but although there were no visible marks on his face, let me show you his body." The doctor then led the way back into the examination room, before pulling back the shroud covering the latest victim.

Rayner looked on as the pathologist indicated a number of bruises to both sides of the rib cage and made specific mention of what looked like faint burn marks on each of the fingers of the right hand.

"What do you make of those, doctor?" the Inspector enquired.

"I have seen similar marks before, and my guess is they were caused by some kind of heated terminals attached to the digitals."

"Such as electrical attachments?"

"Yes, I suspect the victim was electrocuted before he was killed."

"Yet another form of torture?"

"I believe so; the man would have suffered considerably, but similarly to the first victim, there was a strong odour of laudanum coming from his mouth."

"Have you any idea how the bruises were caused to the upper body?"

"The majority appear to have been the result of heavy

punches, but if you look closely at the three lines of discolouration across the left bottom rib, I suspect they were caused by some kind of metal bar or heavy cudgel. But there's more."

The doctor then turned the corpse over, exposing his back and both Rayner and Robinson gasped when they looked upon what appeared to be deep lash marks running across the victim's back.

"My God," the Inspector said, "He'd been birched."

"With a great deal of force being administered, or some kind of leather whip was used which has bitten deeply into the flesh."

"Such as a riding whip?"

"Possibly."

"Can you calculate how old those wounds are?"

"It's obvious they were put there fairly recently. My guess would be just prior to his death." The doctor paused whilst replacing the shroud and then confirmed, "Examining closely the angle at which the knife entered the chest wall, I also believe he was stabbed from behind."

"After being forced to occupy the seat in which he was discovered?"

"Yes, and in answer to your earlier question about the location of the murder, I am convinced he was stabbed in that same seat, the person responsible obviously standing behind him in the next row up."

Rayner's mind returned to the Royal Strand Theatre and the position of the seats inside the auditorium. There was no doubt the killer could have been standing behind the seated victim and thrust the murder weapon down into the man's chest.

After leaving the mortuary, Jack Robinson asked an obvious question. "What kind of man would inflict those sorts of injuries on another? You would have thought that by whipping and striking a victim would have been sufficient, but to electrocute him as well seems abnormal."

"One whose mind has been eaten away by hatred and revenge Jack, I suspect over a long period of time."

Richard Rayner spent that evening with his wife at home, discussing various aspects of their recent experiences at both the college where Clarice worked, and Scotland Yard. The man of the house explained that he suspected race meetings in particular were prominent features, and could be an important common denominator in the Inquiry into both murders. His suggestion prompted Clarice into remembering the information shared by the student Grimes, during the lecture she had delivered earlier that day, encouraging her to report the details to her husband.

"I was most surprised Richard when he told me his father had a horse kept at his stables which was apparently a fancied runner for this year's Derby. Someone must have broken into the stables last night and somehow managed to drug the local stable boy who was paid to watch over that particular horse, before it was taken."

"What was the horse's name?" her husband asked, inquisitively.

"Fleet of Foot; have you heard the name?"

"No, but I shall ask Henry, knowing he follows horse racing when he has the opportunity. I take it that the local constabulary will be making the necessary enquiries?"

"I suppose so Richard, but I'm afraid I didn't bother to get the name of the stables or the location. Do you wish me to do so?"

"If you could dear, it might be worth looking at from the perspective of our current investigation."

Henry Bustle was already waiting in the Inspector's office when Rayner arrived the following morning.

"Good morning Henry, and what have you?"

"Good morning sir, I'm afraid this Thomas Wake is proving to be quite an elusive character."

"Tell me more; what have you actually managed to find out so far if anything?"

"As Miss Pritchard told us sir, the boy left the Upper Clapton Workhouse in 1850 and was moved to the workhouse in Lambeth where his sister, Emily Wake resided. Yet, he was only there for a matter of a few months before being transferred again to an Institution in Woking. According to the records, Thomas received some corrective training there over a three-year period, before he left and appears to have disappeared from sight."

"I take it there is no record then of where he went to, after leaving Woking?"

"According to the Administrator there, at the age of twelve, he is believed to have been employed by a blacksmith by the name of Harbidge in Leyton Buzzard, but alas that individual closed his business in 1854 to join a regiment, and is believed to have been killed in action. There is no record of what happened to Thomas Wake after that."

"What of his sister, Henry?"

"Ah, now she was an easier proposition to track down. Again, according to the records, Emily remained at the Lambeth Workhouse until she reached her sixteenth birthday, when she was moved out to work in service with a family by the name of Grainger who resided near to Cheveley in Cambridgeshire. I still have to make further enquiries there and for all I know, Emily could still be working for the same family and might be able to point us in the direction of her brother's whereabouts."

Richard Rayner sat back in deep thought, taking heed of what Henry Bustle had uncovered, considering a number of aspects. He then leant forward and asked the Sergeant, "Do we know how far Cheveley is from Newmarket?"

"Not far, I think about four miles, certainly within walking distance."

"And Newmarket is about sixty or so miles from London."

"If you say so sir."

"Have you any recollection of a race horse by the name of Fleet of Foot Henry?"

"That particular horse is a three-year old which is fancied for the Derby this year sir. I know she's been out on a few occasions and is yet to be beaten."

"Therefore, to a thief she would be worth a lot of money?"

"Only if the horse could be sold on sir. The racing community is very close knit and such a horse as Fleet of Foot would be easily recognisable, making an illegal sale virtually impossible."

"I take your point Henry which also indicates that the possible motive would be to prevent the horse from running in the Derby, rather than being stolen for monetary gain."

"If the favourite was taken by a competitor who also had a ride entered in the Derby, then the motive would be for monetary gain, eventually."

"Ah yes, I hear what you are saying."

Rayner then disclosed what Jack Robinson had discovered in relation to the background of Elias Thompson, emphasising the fact that both Thompson and Grimbold had been followers of the turf.

"And you suspect that horse racing could be an important feature in their murders sir?"

"It's possible Henry, but at the moment it could be mere coincidence, but everything appears to be pointing towards the gentlemen's sport involving race tracks. I would be interested in accompanying you to Cheveley to find out what eventually happened to Emily Wake. I am beginning to find this part of the Investigation more and more meaningful."

"A Pie-man involved in horse racing?"

"Possibly."

"Shall we be travelling by horse and carriage or train sir?"

Rayner smiled and confirmed, "Your favourite mode of transport Henry, horse and carriage. We shall leave this very morning. Go and fetch your overnight bag."

Both detectives kept a spare set of clothing and other requirements necessary in case they needed to travel and stay away from London overnight, and whilst the Sergeant was retrieving his from his personal locker, Rayner studied a map to find the quickest route to the village of Cheveley. Within an hour they were both leaving the capital in a horse and carriage, heading south.

Chapter Eight

Frederick Morgan loved his job and position as Head of the Detective Branch at Scotland Yard, but on occasions felt a great deal of frustration from being tied down to a desk. Apart from running his department by supervising his detectives, whose general office was on the ground floor and distributing reports of crimes to individual officers, he also had to frequently brief the Commissioner on various topics of interest to the highest-ranking officer in the Metropolitan Police.

Sir Edmund Henderson rarely interfered with the investigative side of Morgan's domain, except when there were unusual circumstances surrounding the commission of a fairly high-profile felony or felonies. The two murders committed apparently by the same deviant, and the amount of time being allocated to them by the newspapers was an exception to such non-interference. As a result, the Superintendent was summoned to visit the top floor suite of offices on a daily basis. Having just delivered the latest briefing and update to the Commissioner, Morgan returned to his office feeling a little annoyed at just being accused of dragging his feet with the investigation into the Grimbold and Thompson investigations.

Having removed his jacket, he stood peering out of his window at nothing in particular, but sensing a burning desire for the same satisfaction he used to experience as a young detective chasing around the backstreets of London in search of information. Morgan had first joined the department at a time when structured criminal investigation was still in its infancy. He was raised on the philosophy that if you couldn't beat a confession out of a suspect, he was innocent. Of course, he still believed in such tactics but with the evolvement of more subtle approaches towards evidence collation, as practiced by detectives such as Richard Rayner, there were occasions when the Superintendent felt that the strategies of the past were becoming more obsolete. What he desperately needed was to achieve more from his own perspective of investigative success, and pondered on the belief he had that the most recent killer his Inspector was seeking, was connected in some way with the workhouses from which the victims had been a part of. Furthermore, in Morgan's mind was a strong suspicion that the man responsible was, as he had already inferred to Rayner, a person who delivered bakery items to those same establishments.

Finally, he decided to act unilaterally, if only to show those junior officers who doubted his ability that Frederick Morgan was still capable of locking up offenders. The time had come for the man from Porthcawl to lead the way, and after summoning his private driver left Scotland Yard via the back door, before instructing the constable holding the reins of the horse and carriage to take him to the Upper Clapton Workhouse.

He was met at the front door by non-other than Nellie Pritchard who he asked for the name and address of the baker who provided supplies to the business.

"Has Inspector Rayner sent you Superintendent?" the lady enquired.

"Inspector Rayner works for me and doesn't send me anywhere," he snapped back at the woman, obviously aggrieved by her suggestion.

"Allow me a moment or two Superintendent," the amicable lady requested, before leaving her visitor standing in the reception staring back at an inquisitive old man with grey hair, who appeared bemused by Morgan's posture and ebony cane he was using to support his frame.

"Fine weather we've been having," the elderly receptionist croaked, with a surly grin, obviously trying to gain some rapport with the senior detective from Scotland Yard.

"It's been pissing down with rain for the past week," the Superintendent impatiently answered, bringing the short conversation to an abrupt end.

When Miss Pritchard returned, she furnished the detective with the name of Joseph Huffman Bakers, 35, Southwark Street near to Blackfriars Bridge Road, Newington.

"Does this particular baker supply meat pies to the workhouse?" Morgan asked.

"I suppose so, but I can enquire with the cook if it's important Superintendent."

"No, that will not be necessary miss, I will bid you good day," he said, before leaving to climb back into his carriage.

"The Christchurch Workhouse in Newgate Street next Percy," he instructed his constable driver before the vehicle took off in the right direction.

Upon arriving at his next destination, Morgan followed the same procedure as before, only this time speaking to a young maid who left him standing on the front doorstep whilst she went to make the necessary enquiries.

It was the Housekeeper of the workhouse where Elias Thompson had been engaged, Alice Entwhistle, who returned to assist the Superintendent.

"Might I ask for what reason do you require the name of our supplier of bread sir?" she politely asked.

"No," Morgan answered, not so politely, "The name and address if you please."

The lady shrugged her shoulder, a little taken aback by her visitor's abrupt manner and informed him of the same name and address given previously by Nellie Pritchard.

Morgan's eyes lit up when he realised the same baker served the same two workhouses in which the two murder victims had been associated and, as before, he asked whether meat pies were ever purchased from the same bakery supplier. Unfortunately, as a result of what the lady regarded as a rude and aggressive manner, the information he sought was not forthcoming, and Alice Entwhistle suggested he should make enquiries with the baker himself.

"That's exactly what I intend upon doing but I find it difficult to thank you lady for the miniscule help you have provided towards the investigation into two murders," he declared, obviously hoping for some kind of shock reaction in response to his insulting remarks, but none was forthcoming and the manageress slammed the door in his face.

"Bleedin' overpaid harlot," Morgan mumbled under his breath, as he returned to his carriage, "Thirty-Five Southwark Street Percy and in all haste," he bawled at his driver, so loud the horse jumped forward almost running a back wheel over the Superintendent's foot. But it all mattered for nothing. He sat inside the vehicle as it moved quickly through the streets of London, glibly satisfied he had moved the Investigation nearer to the point where an arrest was imminent. That was a characteristic feature about Frederick Morgan, or so he told himself, once he got the bull by the horns, the detection rate would soar. He allowed himself a smile, thinking of the look on Richard Rayner's face when he told the Inspector the killer was downstairs in the cells.

Joseph Huffman's bakery was a small establishment with the name of the proprietor painted across a large window, and Morgan ordered his constable to stop just short of the front door to the premises. Having then climbed down from the carriage he ordered his man to accompany him.

"I feel it in my bones Percy, that we are about to put an end to these killings," he told him, boastfully, but Percy was having nothing to do with it, explaining that he wasn't allowed to leave the horse and carriage unattended.

"On whose blood instructions is that?" the Superintendent angrily demanded to know.

"The Commissioner sir. It's always been the case that we drivers are not allowed to leave the horse and carriage unattended, no matter what circumstances prevail."

"I don't give a shit about prevailing circumstances Percy, tie that bloody nag up to that lamp post and follow me. You my son are about to get your name in the history books."

"She's not a nag sir with respect, Daisy is only three years old and needs looking after," the constable obstinately replied, inviting the full wrath of the man armed with an ebony walking cane.

Morgan's face reddened and he exhaled loudly before demanding, "Move your arse constable and do as you have been ordered, or you and that bloody
nag, Daisy, will be keeping each other company outside the soup kitchens."

Constable Percival Jakeman shrugged his shoulders and

surrendered the high ground, not wishing to enter into mortal combat with the Head of the Detective Branch. Having tied Daisy to the lamp post indicated by the Superintendent, he followed Morgan through the front door of the bakery.

"I take it you've got a pair of handcuffs with you?" the senior man quietly asked.

"Always," the constable confirmed.

Joseph Huffman was a large man in his forties with close cropped ginger hair, the same colour as Frederick Morgan's but unlike the senior detective, who spoke with a Welsh accent, the bakers was of local origin. They found him standing behind a small counter working with what seemed to be half a ton of flour used to cover trays of meat pies and other pastries laid out on large trays. Two other, much smaller men, were working in the open baking section of the business premises, which contained two ovens lit and being used to bake whatever products had been placed inside them. Upon hearing the officers enter his shop, the huge frame wearing a large apron covered in white flour, turned and approached them, holding a metal measuring container in one hand. His sleeves were rolled up and both arms were covered in white dust.

"Can I help you gentlemen?" he asked in a deep voice.

"I think you'll find that we can help you Mr. Pie-man," Morgan announced with a confident look across his face, "We've come to tell you we found the pies you left at the Royal Albert Hall and at the Royal Strand, together with those men you gruesomely murdered."

The Baker froze, looking as though he had just entered a nightmare involving Revolution Square and a guillotine in the French capital.

"I do not understand gentlemen, is this a prank and you have been sent by my third cousin Priestley who is the most immature prat in my family?"

"You know bleedin' well it's not a prank Mr. Huffman." Morgan then finally introduced himself and Constable Jakeman, before asking, "Where were you during the night before the last?"

The baker remained looking totally confused, but before answering the question gasped, "Are you accusing me of murdering those two men who have been in the papers? I cannot believe this is happening. I am a baker you red headed baboon, working for an honest living. Where has this all come from?"

Morgan thought it was a bit rich, the baker making light of the colour of his hair which was the same as his.

"You can take the piss out of me all you want Mr. Pie-man," he said with authority, "But answer the question, where were you the night before last?"

"At home with my missus," the disbelieving man quickly replied, "Where I always am every night. Show me your identity cards; this is a prank and I believe my third cousin is behind it."

"In that case, I'm arresting you for the murders of Claude Grimbold, late of the Upper Clapton Workhouse and Elias Thompson, late of the Christchurch Workhouse."

"You are still joking I see. Now enough of this foolhardy business, I have deliveries to make."

"Percy," Morgan quietly said, signalling for the constable to put his issued handcuffs to good use. Before the baker knew what was happening both his hands were bound together inside the manacles.

"I said this has gone far enough," he roared out, "I have deliveries to make."

"So have we," Morgan said, "Straight to the cell block at Scotland Yard."

As the conversation between the two men had been ongoing, the other two employees had been listening at the back of the premises with interest, glancing across at each other every time they heard the Superintendent verbally make his accusations.

Both men were naturally stunned at discovering their employer was a cold bloodied killer. The two men stood motionless as they watched the baker being hustled out of the shop in handcuffs, wondering what they should do with all the loaves of bread, pies and tarts already waiting to be delivered to a list of paying customers. But there was suddenly another hurdle for Frederick Morgan to overcome.

Once out on the pavement, people began to stare across at the sight of a large bulk of a man wearing a tent-like apron covered in flour, and two other official looking gentlemen grasping each of the man's arms, which meant that Morgan needed to get the prisoner away from there as soon as possible before attracting too much attention. The only problem the Superintendent had was the horse and carriage were nowhere to be seen.

"Where is it Percy?" he asked with a concerned voice.

"Probably nicked sir," the constable answered, "I did say the Commissioner had instructed us…"

"Shut yer mouth and go and find the bleedin' thing."

By the time the three men had walked all the way back to Westminster, resembling an act from the famous Barnum's

Circus, they finally arrived at Scotland Yard and the Superintendent instructed Constable Jakeman to take the complaining baker to the cell block. He needed some solace, away from observing eyes. Frederick Morgan's daring escapade was beginning to falter. A wave of potential embarrassment was beginning to build up a head of steam, and he began to urgently think of ways to shift the blame for having lost an official police horse and carriage, at the same time having possibly made a false arrest.

As he stood in his office, wiping off flour from his clothing which had come from his prisoner's apron, his nightmare began to peak when the door was opened and there stood the Commissioner, Sir Edmund Henderson.

"Any joy yet Frederick?" the top man asked.

"Oh yes sir," Morgan sheepishly answered, "But we've met up with one or two slight difficulties."

Chapter Nine

Cheveley was a small, typically English picturesque village, consisting mostly of a few individual cottages surrounded by vast areas of agricultural farmland. The Peacock Inn was the largest building to be seen and next door was a Livery, where the two visitors from Scotland Yard decided to visit first. After leaving their horse and carriage in the care of the local hostler, they entered the neighbouring refreshment house. It was mid-afternoon and apart from a couple of locals playing dominoes and indulging in a tankard of ale each, the bar room was virtually empty.

Richard Rayner made the introductions in his usual panache manner to a tall, muscular landlord with thinning dark hair, who had been called from the back of the premises.

"And what can I get you gentlemen?" the amicable man asked, in a broad countryfied accent indicating he came from

Gloucestershire.

"Two rooms for the night if you please landlord," the Inspector requested.

"That's all we have sir, but they are both vacant at present. How long do you intend staying with us?"

"Just for one night at present, but we shall pay in advance."

The unexpected offer quickly brought a smile to the landlord's face and without further ado, he produced a small ledger from beneath the bar, inviting his two guests to register, which Rayner did on behalf of them both.

"Welcome to the Peacock gents, and what will you be having to quench your thirst?"

"Two glasses of your finest black ale landlord, and perhaps some information," the Inspector requested.

"I can most certainly serve you with the ale," he said, beginning to fill the glasses with drink from a large jug, "But I'm not so sure about the information. What is it you wish to know?"

"The location of Sir Samuel Grainger's residence, if you could direct the way for us?"

"Ah, you have an interest in the sport of champions then sir?"

"Only in the gentleman I have just mentioned."

The landlord leant across the bar and lowered his voice, not that anyone else was within earshot and explained, "Gents, when you leave here, you can journey in any direction north of the village and you will come across any of Sir Samuel's acreage. The stables are situated just a mile or so outside the village, just follow the main thoroughfare and you cannot miss it."

"What about the main house, is that close by to the stables?"

"Aye, you can see it on top of an incline from the stud itself."

"Thank you, landlord."

"Are you looking at buying or selling some stock sir?" The inquisitive man was typical of a nosy village landlord, constantly in search of snippets of gossip to pass on to those of his customers who he deemed to be willingly receptive.

"Neither," Rayner answered, leaving the man to guess what the nature of their business was, whilst leading the way to a table in the far corner, with Henry Bustle bringing up the rear and carrying the drinks.

"Do you intend visiting the residence today sir?" the Sergeant asked.

"I see no reason why not Henry. The sooner we learn what happened to Emily Wake the better. If she's no longer here then it would be pointless in staying."

After finishing their drinks, and bidding the landlord a

temporary farewell, Richard Rayner wasted little time in following the directions given. Both men stepped it out along the narrow country lane with high hedgerows on either side. As they strode past each farmgate the Inspector admired the beauty of the surrounding countryside, taking the occasional deep breath.

"I should think this was an enjoyable change of environment during the time our girl worked here," Bustle remarked.

"Yes, I agree, it's a complete contrast to the dismal and rigorous life involved inside a London workhouse Henry."

The stables occupied a large area of land with its cobbled yard surrounded by stalls, each containing a thoroughbred horse and Rayner counted twenty-five enclosures in total. As the landlord had explained earlier, from where they were standing, they could see the large turreted house sitting on top of a nearby hill, looking down on the stables, in similar fashion to a mother hen watching over her chicks. As the two visitors began to head in that direction, a high-pitched male voice called out to them.

"Can I be of any help gents." A small, middle aged man appeared with a young lad at his side. Both were wearing large floppy caps, britches and knee-high boots. The man gave the impression he disliked the idea of strangers walking around, which was after all, private property.

"Ah yes, and who might I be addressing sir?" Rayner asked with a guarded smile.

"And who might you be sir, and state your business," the man demanded, authoritatively.

"Our business will be revealed to Sir Samuel Grainger alone, but I will most certainly inform you that we are detectives from Scotland Yard, here on official business." Rayner produced his identity card, and then enquired, "So, again, who am I addressing?"

"Jack Lashley, the stable manager and this is young Nicholas one of the stable boys. So, it's Sir Samuel you've come to see; is he expecting you?"

"No, I am afraid we are here unannounced."

"Then I shall escort you up to the house," the stable manager declared, before turning to the boy and requesting, "Keep an eye on her Nick, and make sure she gets no more oats until I say so."

The boy nodded and immediately ran off, before entering one of the stalls on the far side.

"You have a horse with some ailment I gather," Rayner remarked, as all three made their way along a narrow path leading to the house on top of the hill.

"Aye, it's nothing serious though, just a touch of cholic. She'll be as right as rain for the morning run."

"How many horses has Sir Samuel in his stud?" Bustle asked.

"At the moment just twenty, but we're concentrating on getting just two fit for the Derby and during that time the others are just given light training."

"Do you train them in addition to running the stables Mr. Lashley?"

"Heavens no, there's two trainers employed to do that and they are both demanding people. But when one of our horses becomes a winner, then it all seems to have been worthwhile. Here we are gents," the manager said, as they approached the front door, "If you stay here a spell, I'll inform the master of your presence." Jack Lashley quickly left them and disappeared around the side of the building.

"It's a funny thing Inspector," Bustle said, "But this house is not so dissimilar to any of the workhouses in London."

"I fear you are wrong Henry," Rayner answered, with a quiet chuckle, "There is a Venetian influence in the architecture of this building; note the tall narrow windows and pointed turrets with the red relief brickwork interrupting the off-white background. This structure was undoubtedly designed by a true professional architect who I imagine would have come at a very expensive price, unlike the dilapidated old farm houses converted for use as workhouses."

"I can only accept what you say, Inspector."

The surrounding gardens were also broken by stone paths matching the colour of the brickwork of the main house and paid homage to Venetian styled fountains and a rose garden at the side, where the stable manager had disappeared.

Master Lashley then appeared once again at the front door, with a butler standing at his side.

"This way gents," he called, waving an arm.

Both detectives entered a square shaped hall with an open staircase leading off it, before being escorted into a small library containing shelves of books and various framed paintings of race horses adorning its walls. The whole room evidenced the fact the owner of the house was involved in raising and training thoroughbred race horses.

"Lady Grainger will be with you in a moment," the manager said, before once again disappearing from sight, closing the library door behind him.

Above a fireplace containing burning logs, was a large portrait of one particular horse with the legend, "Forest Gate – Derby winner' engraved in the bottom of the frame.

"It appears that Forest Gate was a treasured favourite of Sir Samuel's in the past," Rayner observed.

"She was a filly and I remember her well," Bustle confirmed, "It must be a good ten years or so since she ran her last race."

The lady of the house was middle aged, slim and having obviously retained her youthful looks was still pleasant on the eye, boasting the figure of a woman much younger. She had light fair hair pinned up and her smile was intoxicating, as she apologised for the absence of her husband.

"Sir Samuel is currently at Newmarket and I'm afraid I have no idea when he will be back, but perhaps I can help you gentlemen," she said in a cultured voice, holding out a hand for both visitors to shake.

"Please," she said invitingly, "Take a seat."

The detectives sat on a sofa facing the fire, whilst Lady Grainger gracefully sat in an upright posture on an armchair at the side of them.

Rayner explained the purpose for their visit and outlined the way in which they had traced a girl by the name of Emily Wake to the house where she was supposed to have worked in service, after being moved from the Lambeth Workhouse in London.

"Do you remember the girl, Lady Grainger?" Rayner quietly

asked.

"Have you been offered any refreshments Inspector?" the woman answered with a question.

"No ma'am, but we have just participated before coming here. We are staying at the village Inn in Cheveley."

"Excellent."

"Miss Emily Wake ma'am, she would have been just sixteen when she was supposed to have arrived here. Can you remember the girl?"

"I apologise Inspector, your enquiry about this girl appears to be one of some importunity. Might I ask the reason why?"

"We believe she might be in a position to assist us with a number of serious incidents committed in London ma'am."

"Is she a suspect for whatever these incidents were?"

"No ma'am, just a possible witness. Can you remember the girl working here?" Rayner asked, repeating his question and beginning to feel the lady of the house was reluctant to speak of Emily Wake. But his suspicion was unfounded.

"I most certainly do Inspector, and an excellent maid she became. In fact, Emily is still with us."

Rayner's face lit up and he was about to enquire if he could possibly speak with the girl, who would now of course be a fully-grown lady, when their hostess continued, confirming some stunning news.

"However, she no longer works for us as a maid. She is my daughter-in-law Inspector and resides here with us together with our son, Roland and their two children."

The Inspector couldn't hide the look of astonishment on his face and for a moment remained speechless. The fact that Emily Wake had actually married into the family came as a complete and unexpected surprise.

A patient Lady Grainger paused, retaining that graceful smile and allowing an opportunity for the detectives to re-compose themselves, until Richard Rayner apologised for his lapse in the conversation, and continued to confess, "Actually, we are looking to interview her brother, Master Thomas Wake, who we are also trying to locate."

The lady nodded and smiled, before asking, "Might I ask the reason why you wish to speak with Emily's brother?"

"Please forgive me, but I am not at liberty to disclose that information, except to say we are investigating a number of serious matters which took place in London over the past week or so."

"My my, Inspector, it does all seem to be so mysterious, but perhaps I can help you further. Tom Wake, Emily's brother, is employed by us as our first-choice jockey and attends at the stud early every morning to take out Green Eyes, our most treasured mount and which is highly fancied to win this year's Derby."

Rayner felt a sensation of optimism sweep over him, suddenly remembering what Clarice had divulged to him on the previous evening, concerning the missing race horse from one of her student's father's stables.

"I am by no means anything more than a complete novice when it comes to matters of the turf Lady Grainger, but I do understand that a horse by the name of Fleet of Foot was the favourite for this year's Derby."

"I have heard of the name Inspector," the lady confessed, "But my husband will be in a far better position to enlighten you further on the racing community. But I can tell you we have ploughed a lot of investment into Green Eyes and most of our people truly believe we have a winner on our hands."

Rayner had a distinct feeling the woman was fencing with him; deliberately holding some information back. She gave the appearance of being extremely cagey. Although she had been quite open about the position of Emily Wake and her brother, somehow, he sensed she was undertaking some kind of hidden inquisition by the kind of questions she was throwing back at him. Her voice sounded amicable enough, but her eyes were telling a different story, and he suspected she used her smile to disarm any opposition. He became wary and cautious that the over playing of his hand would be detrimental to what they were trying to achieve.

Finally, he asked, "Could you provide us with Thomas Wake's current address ma'am?"

"I'm afraid I do not have it at present Inspector. You see my husband deals with that side of the business and I know little about the personal details of any of our jockeys and trainers."

"Perhaps I could speak with your daughter in law then?"

"Again, alas I cannot help you. I am sorry, but both Emily and Roland are away visiting but I do expect them to return tomorrow if you could possibly call back."

Rayner stood and nodded at the lady, declaring that he would not use up any more of her time, before thanking her for her co-operation.

"Please call upon us again Inspector whenever it is convenient," she said, pulling on a bell rope hanging down the side of the large open fireplace.

After being showed the front door by the butler, Rayner led

the way back down through the stables until reaching the lane along which they had earlier followed from the village. The sky had darkened considerably and it appeared that rain was imminent. As soon as they were out of sight of the Grainger house and stables, he moved into a field and stood hidden from view behind some thicket, with Henry Bustle perplexed by what they were doing.

"What did you make of Lady Grainger, Henry?" he asked.

"I had the distinct feeling she was only prepared to tell us so much Inspector, and that there was much more she was holding back. I think the purpose for her reluctance was to gain some time to discuss our visit with others."

"Exactly Henry, I felt the same way about the lady, but let's just wait and see if my supposition is correct."

"What supposition sir?"

Chapter Ten

Within a few minutes of reaching their position of concealment, a misty rain began to fall on the two exposed Scotland Yard men, a signal for Henry Bustle to begin complaining.

"It would help sir," he pleaded, pulling the lapel of his coat up, "If I knew the reason why we are standing here."

"You are about to find out Henry," Rayner whispered, as the sound of a horse's hooves reached their ears, heading along the lane towards them, "Get down man."

They both crouched as the rider approached on a chestnut mare and trotted past the hedge behind which they were hiding. It was Lady Grainger.

"Quick Henry, there's no time to lose," Rayner directed, running out of the field back into the lane. The Inspector continued running towards the village with his Sergeant following at his heels. Eventually, just before they reached Cheveley, the rider disappeared from their sight but only for a short while, and the Inspector overheard Bustle remark anxiously, "We've lost her."

As the cottages appeared in the distance, the rain began to fall more heavily and a sorrowful looking Henry Bustle was beginning to feel more dejected. Both men were saturated but in contrast to the Sergeant's negative attitude, his Inspector remained seemingly impervious to bad weather.

Upon reaching the northern end of the village, Rayner stopped and sought shelter beneath a tree at the side of the lane.

"Over there Henry, outside the first cottage on the left," he indicated.

"It's the same horse."

"Yes, and I do believe we have now discovered where our man Thomas Wake resides."

"Shall we take him now Inspector," Bustle asked, with renewed interest.

"No, I would rather the lady didn't know our movements. Obviously, Master Wake is being informed of our intentions to interview him, as I speak. If he is the man responsible for the two murders back in London, he will immediately make arrangements to depart from this vicinity. If he isn't, then he will remain where he is. In the meantime, I do believe we are both in need of a change of clothing." At that Rayner hastily made his way past the tethered horse, heading towards the nearby Inn with Henry Bustle shuffling behind like a tethered donkey, but looking forward to wearing anything that wasn't soaking wet, as the heavy rain continued to soak them.

"You both look as though you got caught out by that small shower," the landlord commented, as the two drenched visitors appeared in the bar room.

"You call that a shower," Bustle said in reply, looking out of a window at the persistent rain.

"Have our bags been taken to our rooms landlord?" Rayner enquired.

"Oh yes sir, and a fire has been lit in both."

It didn't take long before the visitors to Cheveley village reappeared, both men looking and feeling considerably more comfortable. Henry Bustle was about to order two glasses of warming brandy when he was prevented from
doing so by his Inspector.

"Come Henry, we still have work to do before this day is over."

They immediately decamped from the inn, much to the landlord's surprise, and by the time they returned to the cottage at the end of the village, the horse and its rider had disappeared. Richard Rayner had anticipated such circumstances and in the gloominess of the dusk they could see a dim light shining from inside the downstairs room. The senior man immediately sent his Sergeant to cover the back of the property, just in case Thomas Wake turned out to be a runner. At least it had stopped raining, which kept Henry Bustle's spirits at a more acceptable level.

At first there was no answer to Rayner's loud knock on the door, but then a second attempt resulted in a diminutive man appearing on the doorstep. He was of thin build with a mop of unruly fair hair and a clean-shaven fresh face. His boyish looks gazed out at his caller, looking a little surprised.

"Master Thomas Wake I assume," the Inspector said, before introducing himself, "Might I come in sir, I understand you have been expecting us."

The small man stepped off his front porch to quickly look around and beyond where Rayner was standing.

"My Sergeant is standing in your back garden, if you would be so good as to let him in through your back-door sir."

The man grinned, confirming he did possess a sense of humour, and turned before re-entering his home without saying a word.

The cottage was a two roomed accommodation, one room up

and one down with a tiny kitchen overlooking a back garden. Its occupant had built a blazing log fire in an ancient black painted hearth in the small downstairs parlour. Once he had complied with the Inspector's request and was sitting down opposite his two visitors, Rayner wasted little time in beginning his questioning.

"You are Thomas Wake I take it sir?" he asked.

"You obviously know I am," Master Wake answered, still smiling, "What's this all about Inspector?"

"And I believe you are now a professional jockey in training to ride in the forthcoming Derby?"

The man nodded showing a great deal of pride in his eyes.

"Nellie Pritchard sends her regards and hopes you are in good health. Do you remember the lady?"

Wake chuckled gleefully and confirmed, "Of course; I owe my life to Nellie, how is she? I have often thought of her stuck in that vile place of detention."

"And that sir, is what we wish to know more about. The time you spent at the workhouse in Upper Clapton as a young child."

"What exactly do you wish to know? It was one continuous nightmare from which I still bear the scars on my back from all the thrashings I was made to endure after my mother died." The young man's attitude instantly became sombre as a flood of memories returned to him.

"I apologise for touching on what must have been an extremely painful and traumatic part of your life, and I must admit the story about your demise as a mere child prompted my greatest sympathy for you," Rayner quietly explained, "From what Nellie Pritchard has told us, you must have been subjected to the most horrendous bouts of cruelty imaginable."

"It was more than that sir," Wake explained, "I became a target for them to dish out whatever unpleasantries they wished to bestow upon me, from being frequently birched to having to remain in a freezing cold cellar for days and nights on end with vermin as my bed fellows. Those two bastards who ran that house of horrors both deserved the gallows for what they did to myself and other children at the workhouse."

"I understand fully how you must feel, and how you must have nurtured thoughts of revenge over the years that followed."

"You are quite right Inspector, but it all happened a long time ago and as Nellie used to tell me when she brought me food and drink to help me through my ordeals, time is a great healer."

"Have you never wished for Claude Grimbold to be dead?"

"Many times, but memories fade and with them the intensity

of the ill feeling I held towards both of the Grimbolds."

Rayner stood and placed his back to the fire, before asking, "Are you aware that the man is dead?"

Thomas Wake's initial response was one of genuine surprise, but then he confessed, "I cannot hide my feelings. I can only hope he died from a painful disease which reminded him of all the atrocities he committed in life."

"He was murdered in fact; stabbed through the heart after being badly beaten about his body."

Both Rayner and Bustle looked searchingly into the man's eyes, watching for the slightest sign of falsity and in anticipation of how the killer would respond to such news in an effort to conceal his guilt, but there was none visible.

"What of his perverted wife Inspector, is she still alive?"

"Yes, she is and I suspect without regret at her husband's demise."

"I believe that."

Rayner then asked for a detailed account of the jockey's movements on the night Claude Grimbold was found murdered at the Royal Albert Hall.

"Ah, I now see what this is all about. You think it was me who killed him?"

"The thought had crossed my mind," the Inspector remarked, "Where were you a week last Wednesday evening?"

"I cannot recall exactly, but I rarely miss a night when I am not visiting my sister up at the Hall."

"Which Hall is that sir?"

"The Grainger residence, we refer to it as the Hall. I spend most of my evenings up there and after seeing my sister and the children, usually discuss various aspects of races to come with Sir Samuel, who employs me and pays for this cottage. Before that I used to sleep on the hay with the horses, such is my devotion."

"Is there any way in which we can confirm that was the case on that particular evening?"

"Yes, ask those up at the Hall and they will tell you."

"Do you ever visit the Peacock Inn?" Henry Bustle asked.

"Occasionally, but not very often. Inspector," he said, turning back to Rayner, "My whole life now is concentrated on racing Sir Samuel's mounts. I love horses and have done so for many years. When I became independent, I journeyed to Ireland where I worked hard learning my trade with people who I regarded as the best in the business. It was there I first met Sir Samuel at a stud outside Limerick and he invited me for trials back here. I have never looked back and have a lot to thank him for."

"So, it was a coincidence that your sister, Emily, just happened to have worked for the Graingers as a maid?" Rayner enquired.

"No, following my acceptance by Sir Samuel to ride for him, I learned of a vacancy at the Hall and put my sister's name forward as a possible replacement. She was successful and has since married my employer's son Roland, who is also a jockey."

"But what I understand from Lady Grainger, you are the first choice to ride their most favoured mounts?"

"Your terminology confirms your lack of detailed knowledge of the racing game, but yes that is true, but only because I have been fortunate enough to ride more winners than Roland. In fact, he has still to ride his first."

Rayner regained his seat and leant forward with both hands grasped in front of him. He was beginning to believe that the young man sitting in front of him was an honest and dedicated horse racing jockey, certainly not the kind of man they had been seeking for the murders of two workhouse Administrators.

"To be a top-class jockey, which you obviously are," he said quietly and with a wry smile, "I take it you have to make many sacrifices?"

"Yes, of course, but the biggest concern for both myself and the trainers is weight. I have to constantly keep my weight down to a certain level in order to qualify for the races in which I participate, hence the reason I only occasionally visit the village inn. Early nights and early mornings are the rule of thumb by which many of us live."

"Tell me Thomas, does the name of Elias Thompson ring any bells with you, or the Christchurch Workhouse in Newgate, London?"

"No sir."

"What of a horse by the name of Fleet of Foot. Have you ever heard of that?"

"Fleet of Foot is one of our main competitors for the Derby. She is a filly owned by Sir Neville Grimes at Epsom or so I believe."

"Are you aware she has been stolen from her stable down there?"

"No, and if that is the case, I abhor such treachery. I would rather any ride I was selected for was beaten on the flat, than to chalk up another win as the result of such foul play."

"I believe you young man and apologise for taking up so much of your time. Tell me, what time in the morning will you be expected at the stables?" Rayner asked, gaining his feet once again with Henry Bustle doing the same.

"Five o'clock sir. I rise at four every morning and we leave the yard with the horses to run them at exactly five o'clock."

"Then we shall not delay you any further, and I will hopefully see you there."

After leaving Thomas Wake's cottage, the two detectives sat in the bar room at the Partridge Inn, with a broad smile finally returning to Henry Bustle as he enjoyed the convivial warmth coming from a large fire. The Sergeant was in his element, participating in conversation with Richard Rayner and drinking his usual glass of black ale. Rayner was also relaxed, nursing a welcome glass of Malt Whiskey. Both men were ready for their beds but it was important they exchanged views relating to the events of that day.

"So, Henry, did you believe everything young Thomas Wake told us?"

"Yes, I think so. He seemed to be genuine and his love of horses says a lot for him. I think he was genuinely surprised but not disappointed by the news of Grimbold's callous murder."

"I agree, but still suspect our killer is linked in some way to both Master Wake and the Grainger family. It's too much of a coincidence that both our victims had the same interests in horse racing and our main suspect just happened to be a professional jockey."

"You hold doubts about Thomas Wake then sir?" Bustle enquired, after taking a gulp of ale.

"No, I do not Henry, but I do hold doubts about the environment in which he works."

"It does seem odd that Lady Grainger risked riding over here to warn him of our presence."

"I do not feel that the woman's behaviour is linked with anything more sinister than some kind of paternal concern she holds towards her husband's favourite jockey. No, Henry, I think we need to delve more into both victims' backgrounds. It could be they themselves were linked through companionship and if we could discover the mutual interests they may have shared, I believe we will possibly identify the motives for their deaths and the person responsible."

In Henry Bustle's eyes, Richard Rayner was rarely wrong with his assumptions and beliefs, and the Inspector's theory relating to their current Investigation was no exception. However, the Sergeant did have reservations concerning the earlier attitude of Lady Grainger, suspecting malpractice or even criminality behind her facade. He then made mention of the incidents reported to Scotland Yard concerning the thefts of horses in London.

"Do you think those could in some way be connected with the two murders sir?"

"I doubt it Henry, the theft of working horses must be extremely distant from the stealing of a thoroughbred top-class horse from a racing stud such as that of Sir Neville Grimes at Epson, but I do believe that location is worthy of a visit."

"Before or after the Derby has been run sir?"

Both men chuckled, before finally retiring for the night. It was an early start awaiting them in the morning.

Chapter Eleven

The moon was still reflecting through a break in the clouds when they first saw the movements of silhouettes inside the stable yard. The number of horses gathered was fewer than they had anticipated; about a dozen in total with each rider grasping a mug of steaming liquid. Lanterns shone down on the shiny cobbles from the perimeter of the stables and one or two voices could be heard sharing words of instruction and advice.

The hooves of one horse echoed amongst the sounds of creaking leather. as its rider approached them, having seen the two strangers appearing out of the darkness.

"Good morning gentlemen, do meet Green Eyes, the future winner of the Derby," Thomas Wake cheerfully said, referring to his mount. He was astride a beautiful young filly with alert, glistening eyes and boasting a sleek neck patted affectionately by the young jockey. There was a prominent white flash separating the horse's eyes which distinguished the favourite from the other mounts.

"Good morning to you both," Rayner answered, before Henry Bustle just grunted, having not yet been fully awakened by the bracing air accompanying the coldness of the early morning.

"Is Sir Samuel with you this morning?"

"He should be up at the house," Thomas Wake confirmed, "And doesn't usually join us until daylight."

Rayner looked up towards the top of the hill and could see signs of life from a number of dim lights coming from inside the residence.

"Ready lads, Tom you lead the way lad," Jack Lashley, the stable manager's voice could be heard calling out.

"Perhaps you will still be here when we return," the lead jockey enquired.

"If not, I am sure we shall meet again Tom, in the near future.

At that, the young man sitting astride Green Eyes turned the horse's head and slowly walked it towards the narrow lane, with the others strung out in a line behind him.

"What price to be a jockey or trainer, Henry?" Richard Rayner said, as the race horses casually filed past the two detectives. The Inspector breathed deeply, exhilarated by the freshness of the coming dawn.

"Not for me sir. I'm afraid I wouldn't be cut out for all this early to bed and early to rise stuff."

When the last of the steeds had disappeared, leaving a quiet stillness over the whole of the cobbled yard, the two visitors from Scotland Yard made their way up the incline until reaching the main house.

The same butler they had seen on the previous day answered their knock on the door and immediately invited the detectives inside, before escorting them into the ground floor library. There was a sweet perfumed aroma in the air, which Rayner hadn't noticed the day before. It was familiar to him, but not important.

"Can I offer you tea or coffee gentlemen?" the butler enquired, and both men gave their preference for coffee.

"The master should be down shortly and I will inform him of your visit." The man then left the room, closing the door behind him.

"I wish someone would light this fire," Bustle remarked, staring at the cold dispassionate hearth.

As if his wish had been overheard, a young maid entered the room carrying a bucket filled with logs and nodded at the visitors before quickly moving across to the hearth and building a fire.

She then turned up the gas lamps attached to the walls and left the room. Within a few minutes they were seated in a different atmosphere of cheerful warmth, heat being radiated from the burning logs and reaching every corner of the library.

Henry Bustle commented that it would be interesting to know what kind of business Sir Samuel was involved in, considering all the financial overheads required to be met when running such a large stud.

"Horse racing is his only business I suspect Henry," Rayner answered, "The more races he wins the higher his stud fees when facilitating other enthusiasts' requirements. I would agree with you that the cost of running such an establishment as this must be enormous, but so are the winnings he receives when one of his horses is successful. The Derby for example has been held for almost a hundred years and I do believe the winner's purse now exceeds over two thousand pounds."

"It all sounds extremely risky to me sir."

"So it must be, have no fear of that, but an individual such as Sir Samuel Grainger and a few others in similar positions would take precautions against all

possible difficulties and outcomes..."

"Did I hear my name being mentioned?" a man standing in the

doorway asked. Sir Samuel was a small but robustly built man with greased down thinning brown hair, and a pair of mutton chop whiskers encircling a flushed face. He was wearing a short-quilted house jacket and Rayner noticed a pair of slippers on his feet.

Both men stood whilst the master of the house entered the room to shake hands with each of them, following the Inspector's introductions.

"Have you ordered hot drinks?" he enquired in a gruff voice, which was surprising for such a small man.

Rayner confirmed they had, before Sir Samuel waved an arm for his visitors to resume their seats, he himself preferring to remain standing with his back to the blazing fire.

"I understand you spoke with my first-choice jockey last night gentlemen. I hope you are not intending to take him back to London with you?"

"No sir," Rayner answered, "Your employee is quite safe for now, but the reason we have requested to see you is in connection with the stud owned by Sir Neville Grimes in Epsom."

The racing horse owner screwed up his face upon hearing the name, as if he'd just swallowed a stone from a plum.

"I take it sir you are acquainted with Sir Neville?"

"Acquainted is hardly the word," Sir Samuel growled, "A guarded observer would be a better description Inspector."

"Pray tell me, why is that?"

"The man's a charlatan who purports to be a race horse owner but doesn't believe in the rules of fair play. Grimes will do anything to guarantee racing successes, from offering more money to jockeys riding other more favoured mounts to ride for him; to making false accusations of malpractice supposedly committed by other owners and trainers. He's a disgrace to the sport."

Rayner threw a glance in his Sergeant's direction, surprised by the character description he'd just been given. The young maid who had earlier made up the fire, again entered the room with a tray containing cups and a pot of freshly made Java.

After handing each of them, including Sir Samuel, a cup filled with steaming hot coffee, she quietly left the gentlemen to continue with their conversation.

"Are you aware Sir Samuel that the man has just been the victim of a larceny of one of his thoroughbreds by the name of Fleet of Foot?"

"Bah, knowing the villain as I do, I have no doubt it involves some kind of trickery and I would suggest you look no further for

143

the thief than Grimes himself."

"I understand the horse was a favourite to win this year's Derby, so how would its owner benefit from losing his prize possession?" Rayner asked.

"I've no idea, but I repeat, anything that braggard is connected with, will be cloaked with skulduggery, take my word for it young man."

"I would imagine if that was the case, the potential consequences would be too hideous to contemplate, however, do the names Claude Grimbold or Elias Thompson mean anything to you?"

The Knight of the Realm thought for a moment and then confirmed they did not.

"Finally, could you confirm for us that Thomas Wake was here, in your presence, during the evening of a week last Wednesday?"

"Most probably, young Tommy calls here every night before returning to his cottage. If he had been missing on any night, I would have noticed."

"Thank you, sir, then we shall not detain you any further," Rayner said, getting to his feet.

"Do you think your horse, Green Eyes, is worthy of a flutter sir to win this year's Derby?" Henry Bustle boldly asked, already guessing the answer.

Sir Samuel placed both hands on his hips and leant back as if about to spring forward with some momentum.

"You can put your house on it sir. She will win by at least a couple of lengths, and I promise you this, Green Eyes will not go missing before the race."

At least their journey back to London was a dry one with most of the clouds having dispersed and an occasional glimpse of the sun adding to the pleasure of the trip. Henry Bustle held the reins and commented that he didn't think they were any further forward than before they had left the capital to visit the Cambridgeshire stud.

"I disagree Henry," Rayner argued, "I think we have learned a lot which has made this excursion worthwhile. Remember, as I have mentioned before, our two victims were both interested in horse racing and it would appear they regularly attended meetings. I believe that is too much of a coincidence, bearing in mind the man who was once our principle suspect is now a high-flying jockey."

"But no longer a suspect sir? You didn't feel we warranted talking with his sister?"

"What about Henry? She only came into the equation when we were trying to locate her brother. There was no other reason for us to bother the lady."

Bustle then asked in what direction his Inspector thought the Investigation was going and what would be their next move. The question was a sincere one, the Sergeant having become so immersed in the subject of horse racing and the individuals engaged in the sport, he had lost some of his impulsive thinking regarding other avenues.

Rayner explained that he wanted to talk with Jack Robinson and task him with finding out more about the backgrounds of both Sir Neville Grimes and Sir Samuel Grainger.

"I am not so naïve as to ignore the possibility that either or both of them could have been involved in some kind of shady deals in the past Henry," he explained, "But our next call, after we have spent a night with our families will be Epsom."

"Sir Neville Grimes stables?"

"Yes."

"But I fail to see how that gentleman's business would be linked in any way to either of our murders?"

"Not perhaps the man's interests in the turf, but I sense the theft of his favourite horse might be interesting to look into."

There was a glint in Richard Rayner's eyes, seen many times before, usually present when the Inspector felt he was going along the right track and closing in on the man they were seeking.

When they finally arrived back at Scotland Yard, they were greeted by Superintendent Frederick Morgan who they found to be in a more agitated state than usual. Clouds of blue smoke from his personal bonfire were invading the corridor outside his office, always a sign of some crisis challenging his thought patterns. From the flushed face and concerned look on Morgan's face, Rayner guessed there had been yet another development in the murders they were investigating.

"Whilst you pair have been learning all about placing a wager on the gee gees," he said sarcastically, "Our Pie-man has dispatched his third bleedin' victim."

Chapter Twelve

Both men sat and listened to every detail shared with them by Frederick Morgan. The Superintendent explained that a patrolling constable had found the corpse sitting upright on a bench inside Hyde Park, shortly after Rayner and Bustle had left London on the previous morning. According to the officer he initially thought the motionless figure was that of a sleeping vagrant, until noticing blood down the front of his shirt.

"Do we know who he is?" Rayner asked.

"Not yet, but there's no doubting from his appearance, he is in fact a vagrant." Morgan then went on to describe how he attended the scene with Sergeant Jack Robinson and viewed the body in situ, before Doctor Critchley arrived and confirmed death had been caused by a single stab wound to the chest. The Superintendent explained that a cursory search of the dead man's clothing found nothing that might have helped with any identification. The pathologist calculated the man had been dead for approximately four to five hours.

"How do we know he was the victim of the same killer who dispatched Claude Grimbold and Elias Thompson?"

"Because there was a bloody big meat pie sitting in his lap, Rayner." With a great deal of frustration in his voice, Morgan then described the same kind of
white label found on the base as with the previous two murders.

"The insolent bastard had written the words, 'Where justice would fail, I succeed.' I'm really getting pissed off with these messages Rayner. Is there no way in which these could give us a hint of who this delinquent is?"

The Inspector had already given a great deal of thought to that possibility without coming up with one single positive notion. And yet now, after his recent diversion into the world of horse racing, perhaps there was more they could do.

"The ink used to write the missives is fairly common, so we could not expect much help coming from that angle," he suggested, "But what of the paper, the label used by the writer?"

"I don't follow sir," Bustle confessed.

"What if the labels being used had been stored or handled in some location where various elements might have been transferred on to them, mere specs not visible to the naked eye?"

"A long shot Rayner."

"Yes, it is sir, but one I feel might be worth taking. Where is the third message now?"

"In your desk drawer, together with the previous two."

The Inspector nodded, and Morgan continued to explain that the body was now at the mortuary where the pathologist should have completed the post mortem.

"We shall go there now," Rayner confirmed, "And see what the doctor has for us." He then asked for the whereabouts of Jack Robinson.

"He's at the mortuary with the body."

"Very well Superintendent, we shall brook no further delay. Come Henry, let's see if this victim's injuries are similar to the previous two."

"At least one thing is certain sir, we can now most definitely rule out Thomas Wake as the killer. He was with us at the time this victim met his death," Bustle concluded, soliciting a nod of agreement from his Inspector.

They were greeted at the mortuary by Jack Robinson who informed them that Doctor Albert Critchley was in his office. The young Sergeant then produced a crumpled ticket he confirmed he'd found inside one of the victim's trouser pockets. It appeared to be a laundry ticket issued twelve months previously by a Chinese Laundry situated in Cheapside. The only identifying mark was a faded number located in the top right-hand corner, 3080.

Rayner immediately handed it to Henry Bustle who agreed to visit the laundry without delay, before then scurrying off with some urgency. Then turning to Jack Robinson, Rayner asked, "What other enquiries have been made Jack during our absence?"

"None really sir. I'm afraid we were all dragged into the farcical of trying to prove the Jewish baker's guilt and of course, most of us were sent out looking for the horse and carriage the Superintendent lost in Newington."

"You've lost me Jack. What was all that about?"

The young Sergeant explained briefly about the wrongful arrest of Joseph Huffman and the manner in which Frederick Morgan's horse and carriage was stolen whilst at the time, the senior detective was making his arrest inside the bakery.

"We were fortunate sir," Robinson continued, his face looking serious but his eyes displaying some jollity, "We found them in another nearby street and thankfully it appears it was a prank played on us by some of the local urchins, rather than an attempt to steal and sell the transport on."

"What of the baker arrested by the Superintendent?"

"Well, as far as I know sir, he threatened to take some legal action against us for loss of business, but fortunately the Commissioner persuaded him against that idea. There's a rumour going around that the man was paid out a few quid to compensate for any loss of earnings."

Rayner decided he didn't need to know any more about the Superintendent's antics, so just smiled before requesting that Jack Robinson focus on finding out what information he could about the two race horse owners.

"Background information on Sir Samuel Grainger and Sir Neville Grimes is what we are looking for Jack," he clarified, "Look for the kind of businesses they delved into prior to becoming wealthy men and what the official reasons were for them being knighted by the Queen."

"Leave it with me sir, I'll get on it straight away."

After watching Robinson disappear, the Inspector then made his way to the pathologist's office which was adjacent to the examination room.

"What have we doctor?" he asked, seeing the pathologist

seated at his desk.

The man put down a pen used for recording his conclusions and immediately welcomed Rayner in an appreciative manner. It appeared the pathologist was relieved that the Inspector was back in charge, following some friction with Frederick Morgan.

"The Superintendent might already have told you Inspector that the victim died in the same way as the two previous men from a stab wound to his heart."

"Yes, but what of other injuries?"

"Surprisingly none, except for the same burn marks on the fingers of the right hand, the same as were present on the cadaver of Elias Thompson, but there were other aspects dissimilar to the others."

Rayner took a seat and listened intently as the doctor continued with his verbal report.

"The man was extremely emaciated. His stomach contents revealed nothing, which confirmed he hadn't eaten food for at least forty-eight hours. Also, except for the bloodstains on his shirt, there were none at the scene which leads me to suspect he was killed elsewhere, before being left in the park."

"It's been suggested he was a vagrant?"

"Most definitely, but I wish to make one further observation."

The pathologist stood and beckoned Rayner to follow him back into the examination room, before stepping across to one corner where the victim's clothing had been piled up on a stool. Holding up the dead man's jacket the doctor then explained, "Although all of his clothes were well worn, they were of a high quality. The jacket is made of cord and the trousers are lined, not the kind of attire worn by the average homeless wretch."

"It seems then that our victim was once a man of substance, possibly falling on hard times more recently?"

"Yes, and from the condition of his boots, it wasn't that long ago he enjoyed a far better standard of living. The boots are made of the finest soft brown leather although as you can see, they are badly scuffed and have been subjected to a great deal of wear and tear."

Rayner nodded his understanding and then asked to see the burn marks on the victim's fingers, which the doctor showed him after removing the shroud from the corpse lying on the examination table. The Inspector noted how painfully thin the dead man appeared to be; his facial features being hollow and the cheek bones more prominent than was the normal case. He couldn't help but feel sympathetic towards the victim's demise and circumstances.

Examining the burn marks on each of the fingers, Rayner then made his own observations. "I appreciate what you told me before, that you suspected these were made as a result of the victim being electrocuted, and I recall you did mention doctor that you had seen the same kind of markings previously."

"Yes, but only in recent years."

"Describe to me if you can, what is the most likely method a killer would use to electrocute his victim."

"A daunting one Inspector. By attaching leads to the subject's fingers and completing a circuit, all he has to do then is switch on his machine and run a current of electricity through his victim's body. If the voltage applied is too strong it could result in the heart being stopped and of course, instant death. But in this case and that of the previous victim, that was not the case."

"What kind of a machine are we talking about?"

"One which generates electricity, possibly a piece of equipment that contains magnets which when turned produce the desired effect."

"Which I take it would be extremely painful for the subject?"

"Extremely painful, yes."

"What of the administration of laudanum you found on the lips of the previous two victims? Was there any trace with this one?"

"No, which means he wasn't drugged, or some other form of sedation was used which might come to light when the toxicology tests have been made."

"Such as opium or a similar drug?"

"Possibly, but I am inclined to rule out opium at present because that too can leave an odour which I failed to detect."

"Thank you. Could you let me know if any trace of drugs is found in the tests you will be making?"

"Of course."

Before returning to Scotland Yard, Richard Rayner called at Kings College to see his wife, whom he found busy attached to a microscope over her desk. They both embraced and Clarice left her husband in no doubt he had been badly missed during his stay in Cambridgeshire. After quickly exchanging a little gossip, he asked if she had received any further news concerning the larceny of Fleet of Foot from the young student, Grimes.

"No, I haven't seen the young man since my lecture Richard, but I could make some enquiries with him if you so wish?"

"No, that's fine dear, I shall be personally visiting the boy's father shortly, after tying up a few loose ends here in London first." He then told Clarice of what had transpired from his visit to the Grainger stud and the eventual discovery of Thomas Wake, who was now a professional jockey. She was delighted that the young man was no longer a suspect, but then her husband gave her a brief description of the more recent murder in Hyde Park.

"The pathologist is of the opinion that two of our victims were tortured by the use of electricity sourced from some kind of generator, and I was wondering Clarice if you have ever come across such a machine during your research?"

"I haven't Richard, but I've no doubt someone in the Science Block might
very well have done so. I shall ask and see what I can find out."

"A generator isn't the kind of machine you could just purchase from a shop I suspect, and I should imagine building one would require a great deal of knowledge. That tells me the killer could well be connected with some industry or seat of learning whereby such a machine is in use."

"I take your point dear. Leave it with me and I'll try and find out what I can. Will you be coming home this evening or are you planning on a trip to Epsom today?"

"I think an evening at home in your company is too tempting to go gallivanting across the country once again. I think my next excursion can wait until tomorrow."

She smiled, obviously thankful for her husband's

consideration.

"There is one more request I wish to make Clarice. Would you be so kind as to bring one of your microscopes home with you this evening?"

"Yes of course. Does this mean you will be assisting me from now on?"

They both laughed, knowing there was more chance of crossing the Atlantic in a hot air balloon.

When Rayner eventually arrived back at Scotland Yard, he found Henry Bustle waiting in his office.

"What have we Henry?" he asked, hanging his top coat up on the stand near to the door.

"Something that will be of interest to you Inspector," the Sergeant announced, "I visited the laundry in Cheapside and they confirmed the ticket had been issued by themselves. I was impressed by the manner in which they keep records of customers going back years, and that receipt bearing the serial number 3080 was issued on payment for a fairly large order of bed linen to be washed and ironed. But surprisingly, it wasn't issued to any individual. The ticket was issued to a workhouse in Cannon Street, not that far from Cheapside."

Richard Rayner looked astonished and congratulated his Sergeant. "There's no time like the present to go visiting Henry and see if anyone there can possibly throw some light on who our third victim is."

During the journey to Cannon Street, the Inspector briefed Bustle on the post mortem findings of the pathologist and placed some emphasis on the notion that the victim had been tortured by means of electrocution.

"In the same way as that in which Elias Thompson was tortured?"

"Yes, but imagine you intended electrocuting someone Henry, how would you go about it?"

"I haven't the slightest clue about electricity sir, I'm still trying to come to terms with how the gas lamps work."

"Exactly, and I suspect the majority of the population would respond in the same way."

"So, you suspect sir that our killer is in some way connected with an environment in which electricity is prominently used?"

"Or where it is made available for use."

The Cannon Street Workhouse was not so dissimilar in appearance to the other Institutions the two detectives had previously visited. A tall, dismal looking building with heavy wooden double doors at the front, which Henry

Bustle knocked as loudly as he could.

A spindly elderly man with shoulder length white hair and a miserable look on his haggard face answered the call. After Rayner had introduced them both, he requested that he spoke to whoever was in charge, resulting in the old man disappearing and leaving them standing inside a cold, narrow hallway.

The two detectives were kept waiting for some considerable time, before finally a portly looking gentleman with a double chin appeared. He was dressed in a shabby jacket and trousers, and a bright green velvet vest.

Charles Somerville introduced himself as the Administrator of the establishment.

"How can I help you gentlemen?" he offered with a broad grin across his ruddy face whilst rubbing his palms together in similar fashion to a money lender about to collect interest on a debt.

Rayner briefly explained the nature of their enquiries, explaining that they were trying to identify a man who they suspected had been connected with the workhouse in the past. A description of the victim was given.

"I have only held this position for a few months and can

honestly say there is no one of that description working here at present, but if you allow me, I will fetch the House Keeper, Mrs. Rogers, who has been resident here for a lot longer. If anyone should know who your mystery man is, she will."

Again, they were left alone looking at the bare, muddy coloured walls and hoping that their endurance would eventually pay dividends.

Mrs. Rogers was a slightly built woman with grey hair tied up in a bun at the nape of her neck. She certainly looked more austere than the Administrator and spoke with a Scottish accent.

Rayner repeated the description of the latest murder victim to her, and she immediately responded by suggesting it could be the Administrator's predecessor, Mr. Conal Gumbley, an Irishman who was dismissed by the charity for becoming heavily weighed down by debt.

"Have you any idea how Master Gumbley ran up so much debt?" Rayner asked.

"Unfortunately, like most of those from across the water, he succumbed to the evils of gambling, until one day two men called here asking for him. Heaven forbid, they were both debt collectors and only then did we realise how much disgrace Mr. Gumbley had brought on the establishment. He was dismissed forthwith, never to be seen or heard of since,"

Rayner asked if the lady would agree to accompany them to St Mary's to view the body and hopefully make an identification. At first, she was reluctant, but after the Inspector explained how vital her assistance was required in a serious investigation into a triple murder case, she finally agreed.

Within a few minutes, Mrs Rogers had confirmed the body lying on the mortuary slab was indeed the former and disgraced Administrator, Conal Gumbley. When asked if she knew whether the Irishman had shown any tendency towards making wagers on horse racing, she offered her opinion that the man would have bet on the weather or on how many blades of grass there were in her back garden, if he had ever been given the opportunity.

Chapter Thirteen

Jack Robinson was waiting in readiness to deliver his report when Rayner and Bustle returned to Scotland Yard. Frederick Morgan also joined them in the Inspector's office to listen to what progress had been made, but not before making a personal unexpected declaration of intent.

"You will be pleased to know gentlemen that from today I have given up the pipe."

"Thank God for that," Henry Bustle involuntarily blurted out, "I mean, well done Superintendent, you must be very proud?"

"Prides got nothing to do with it Bustle. I've been ordered by the Commissioner to have my office re-decorated at my own expense. Apparently, he objects to the tobacco stains on the walls and ceiling."

The others struggled to stop themselves from laughing out

aloud in front of the Superintendent, and Richard Rayner quickly asked Jack Robinson to wait before delivering his report. Having then wiped his blackboard clean, he began to chalk the names of each of the deceased and the workhouses with which they had been connected.

"As we know, the first victim, Claud Grimbold was the manager of the Upper Clapton Workhouse; Elias Thompson was about to retire from his position as manager of the Christchurch Workhouse, and we now know the latest victim, Conal Gumbley was recently dismissed from his supervisory job as manager of the Cannon Street Workhouse."

"Each of them being or having been, Administrators of workhouses," Bustle confirmed, needlessly and attracting a hostile glance from the Superintendent.

"Which cannot be coincidental," Rayner pointed out, "And furthermore, it appears each of our victims was connected in some way to horse racing."

"How does that intelligence point us towards identifying the killer, Inspector?" Morgan enquired.

"From what we learned from Thomas Wake and the treatment he was subjected to as an orphan sir. When working and residing under the guardianship of the Grimbolds', it might just be possible there were other young boys treated in the same way as Master Wake."

"You believe the motive behind all three murders is one of revenge?"

"Yes, what we are looking for is a child who, at the time each of our victims remained in their positions at those Institutions, was resident at all of the three workhouses involved in our investigations."

Rayner then finally turned to Jack Robinson and requested the young Sergeant to share what information he had gleaned.

The young man took the floor and being the only person present standing, explained, "Beginning with Sir Samuel Grainger sir, before purchasing the stud at Cheveley he was a highly successful trainer and for a period was commissioned as the principle trainer at the Royal stables at Buckingham Palace. In fact, he served both Queen Victoria and Prince Albert."

"Hence the reason for his Knighthood," Morgan remarked.

"Yes sir, but obviously he made his fortune during that same period from his various commissions which accompanied his position."

"By honest deeds or otherwise," the Superintendent inferred accusingly.

"There is no evidence or supposition supporting any alleged malpractice by Sir Samuel. It would appear he has always had a reputation for being completely trustworthy and honest sir," the young Sergeant said, in answer to the Superintendent's throw away remark.

"What of Sir Neville Grimes, Jack?" Rayner enquired.

"He is a different kettle of fish altogether sir," Robinson confirmed, reading from his open notebook, "He was born and raised in Whitechapel and as a youngster was sentenced to three years hard labour for having stolen a diamond ring from a jeweller's in Covent Garden. Following his release from Newgate Prison, he then worked as a barrow boy in Smithfield Market before the records offer no more information, until a few years later when he suddenly re-appeared on the social scene as a trainer for a stud in Northamptonshire."

"Was he successful in that position Jack?"

"Only in escaping from justice following an altercation involving the killing of a man during a public house brawl in Whitechapel, for which he was arraigned before The Queen's Justice's, but later acquitted."

"Do we know the reasons for that acquittal?" the Inspector asked, enthusiastically.

"No sir, but it was just after that particular court appearance that Sir Neville went to ground again, until ten years ago he suddenly came to notice in the London Telegraph having purchased his present stud at Epsom. Since then he has quite openly courted the press, informing them of a string of charities he subsidises, including two in particular for which Her Majesty is the patron."

"Now we know why *he* was given a knighthood," Morgan remarked with some sarcasm, "Men who purchase their Knighthoods are not worthy of the title."

"What do we know about the larceny of the horse, Fleet of Foot, Jack?"

Robinson explained that he had communicated by telegram with an Inspector Shoreditch who was leading the Investigation, and the reply told him merely of the basic facts surrounding the crime.

"It appears they have no real leads as to the whereabouts of the thoroughbred or the identity of those responsible for the felony sir."

Henry Bustle then asked a question as to why Richard Rayner had so readily dismissed any notion of Sir Samuel Grainger being behind the unlawful taking of the horse.

"We both heard the bile in Sir Samuel when he spoke of Sir Neville Grimes sir, and who would have a stronger motive to cause such grief to his main opponent than Sir Samuel?"

"I suspect Henry, the removal of such a horse from its enclosure in the middle of the night and subjecting the steed to whatever measures are required to keep it concealed, would amount to a certain amount of cruelty. You saw the framed portraits of horses in Sir Samuel's house and I got the impression the man thought more of his steeds than he did his wife. I do not believe he is the kind of man to put any horse through that kind of discomfort and trauma. Considering what Jack has told us about Sir Neville Grimes, if the boot was on the other foot I might well be thinking differently."

"So, what's your next move Inspector," the Superintendent asked, slouching back in his chair with both arms folded across his chest, and obviously missing something he could stick between his teeth and suck on.

Rayner explained that he needed Jack Robinson to try and locate records of inmates of all three workhouses mentioned earlier, when each of the murder victims were in occupation, and to see if there is one name which is recorded at all three establishments during the relevant times.

"Myself and Sergeant Bustle intend travelling to see Sir Neville Grimes in his working environment, and perhaps scrutinise the Investigation ongoing into the missing race horse."

"You suspect then that either Grimes or Grainger could be connected in some way to all three murders?"

"No sir, but I do suspect the stolen horse might be."

Rayner then took a railway timetable from one of the drawers in his desk and commented that their destination was only fourteen miles from London.

"Wouldn't you rather journey by horse and carriage for such a short distance Inspector?" Bustle enquired, not really relishing the thought of being dragged along by one of those steam monstrosities.

"Yes I would Henry, so arrange for one to be here first thing in the morning."

A relieved Sergeant smiled his pleasure. There had been two pleasing occurrences during that day; his Inspector's agreement not to travel by rail and the Superintendent's decision to no longer fill the corridor with acrid smoke.

Richard Rayner asked Jack Robinson if he would telegram Inspector Shoreditch, to inform the officer they would be arriving at the village of Epsom at approximately 10.0 am in the morning, and could he meet them at the local livery there.

After dinner that same evening, Rayner retired to his study with a microscope provided by his wife. Producing the three labels recovered from the pastries found at the scene of the murders, he examined each one beneath magnification. What his eyes looked upon was of interest to the Inspector. He could see a number of different marks on each of them, but recognised one discolouration in particular which was present on all three labels. The mark was a faded brown colour, which was visible to the naked eye provided the observer was looking for it. Otherwise it was insipid and innocuous in appearance.

Returning to the parlour where Clarice was seated, quietly studying a number of academic papers on her lap, Rayner asked if it was possible she could try to have the source of the common mark on each of the labels identified.

"Perhaps the scientists at your college could be of assistance," he suggested, "But we must be careful not to disturb any of the handwriting thereon, just in case the samples are of evidential value at a later time."

"I can but try Richard," she answered without looking up, "Leave all three specimens with me and I shall take them to work tomorrow."

Clarice then told her husband of what she had discovered relating to his earlier enquiry regarding electricity generators, explaining that she had visited the Science Laboratories at the college prior to leaving for home.

"Professor Arthur Clifton spent some time working with a pioneer of electricity by the name of Joseph Swan and now conducts research at Kings College. Apparently Mr. Swan is working on some project to do with light bulbs, and much of what the professor told me was difficult for a lay person such as myself to understand Richard. But he did confirm that to generate electricity a number of magnets would be required to create a magnetic field from which the electricity could be extracted."

"Did he mention the probable size of such a machine?" her husband asked.

"Yes, he told me that it would have to be fairly large and would most certainly not be portable. The professor also mentioned that the kind of generator we were discussing would have to be housed inside a building, as water or moisture could be detrimental to the running of such a machine."

"Thank you dear, that is most helpful."

"Have you any suspect yet Richard?"

"No, but I feel that we are drawing closer as each day passes by. Tomorrow will be extremely interesting."

"I also managed to again speak with young Master Grimes and asked for the location of his father's stud. He told me it can be found in between Epsom and Elwell, if that's any help to you?"

"It most certainly is dear, again thank you."

The detectives made good time in reaching the village of Epsom, and Rayner brought the carriage to a halt outside a small livery at the northern end of the location. It was a sunny day with no sign of rain, and as the detectives prepared to step down from their vehicle, a tall, average built man in a bowler hat, wearing a brown mackintosh, approached them.

"Inspector Shoreditch I take it?" Richard Rayner enquired.

"George Shoreditch at your service gentlemen, your reputation comes before you Inspector Rayner and it is an honour to meet you sir." The local Inspector was a clean-shaven youngish man with a fresh face and pleasant smile.

"Thank you," Rayner answered, "Once we have seen to our horse and carriage would you be so kind as to take us to Sir Neville Grimes estate."

"Of course. I've arranged for old Henry, the local hostler to take care of your horse and I have another open carriage and driver just over the way there. Perhaps I could update you on our Investigation whilst we travel along. It's not far to the stud you wish to visit; just this side of Elwell."

The two Scotland Yard detectives listened with interest to the description of what actions George Shoreditch had taken since the horse known as Fleet of Foot went missing. After concluding his briefing, Richard Rayner was satisfied his counterpart had done all that could be asked of him in the circumstances. It appeared the valuable horse had been led away from its enclosure, towards some open fields to the north of the Downs and a fair distance away from the race course, famous for hosting the Derby each year.

"Apart from Fleet of Foot, was there anything else missing do we know?" Rayner asked.

"Just a piece of rope which was hanging from the wall and which I suspect was used to secure the horse prior to the larceny."

"What of the stable boy who I understand was drugged before the incident took place? Are you satisfied his story is genuine?"

"At first, I was suspicious of the lad, but have no doubt now that something was put into his food. Mavis Jennings, the local maid was in the habit of taking the boy, a lad by the name of Henry Withers, his supper at eight o'clock each evening but on the night the horse was taken there was an unusual incident."

Rayner looked genuinely interested in what he was being told.

"When she had prepared the supper for the stable boy, a man appeared at the kitchen door which is at the back of the main house and informed the girl that he'd been sent by Sir Neville to support Henry Withers. According to the same man, there had been rumours that Fleet of Foot had become the target of thieves. Well, he suggested to young Mavis he could take the covered tray of food to the lad. She asked if he required some refreshments, but he declined, telling her he was to remain inside the enclosure with Master Withers for the remainder of the night."

"And she believed him?" Henry Bustle asked.

"She had no reason to doubt the man's story and thought nothing more about it until the alarm was raised the following morning."

"And I presume Sir Neville knew nothing about this late-night caller?"

"No, he had no knowledge and I suspect whatever drug was used to put the lad to sleep was surreptitiously added to his food or jug of cider that went with it, prior to the stranger making the delivery."

"What was the story he gave to the stable boy when he arrived with the supper?"

"He told the lad he was a friend of the family visiting to inspect the security of the stables, which he intended doing the following day. Again, according to young Henry, the man was extremely plausible and actually advised him to stay awake throughout the night by playing a card game called 'Patience'. He left a deck of cards with the lad before disappearing."

"The audacity of the fellow goes beyond belief," Bustle commented.

"What was the description given to you by both the stable boy and maid?"

"That Inspector, I remember by heart. He was a young man in his middle to late twenties with fair hair and a goatee beard, which both witnesses told me was well trimmed. He had a round face and was wearing dark clothing and what they thought was a black bowler hat, not unlike the one you are wearing Sergeant." Shoreditch indicated Henry Bustle's headwear.

Rayner was pleased that the information shared by George Shoreditch was far more than he had anticipated. As their carriage turned off the lane to enter through two open wrought iron gates, the Scotland Yard man was optimistic. They followed a long narrow driveway and after a few hundred yards, a large red bricked building sitting halfway up an incline came into view. It uncannily reminded the visitors of the location of Sir Samuel Grainger's house near to Newmarket.

The visitors entered the stables area and were surprised to see a man dressed in riding britches and boots struggling with one of the horses. The man wore a tweed jacket and deerstalker hat and was bellowing out all kinds of obscenities at the obviously fearful animal.

"Ah, I see Master Swain is having to instil some discipline into one of the mounts. He's Sir Neville's stable manager and a bit of a disciplinarian with both horses and riders," George Shoreditch explained.

As their carriage came to a halt, Henry Bustle couldn't fail to notice a look of intense anger on the Inspector's face. When the same disciplinarian struck the horse across its front flank with a whip, Richard Rayner leapt from the carriage and charged across the yard, before yanking the whip from the man's grasp and pushing him to the ground.

"You are a disgrace sir," he yelled at the fallen stable

manager, "For a man who is supposed to be in charge of these animals I find your behaviour both cruel and unnecessary."

Sir Neville's employee smirked and spat back, "I don't know who you are mister but you are about to get your arse kicked all over this yard."

At that, Rayner used the same whip on its owner, striking him twice across his chest, before flinging it to one side.

"That's a dose of your own medicine," the Inspector said, having watched the man cringe beneath the lash.

The horse which had been subjected to the over indulgent beating bolted from the yard and disappeared from sight, as Rayner stood over his opponent with both hands on his hips.

"Well then Mr. Swain, I deplore bullying tyrants such as yourself, so do please oblige me by getting to your feet and fulfilling your threat." The fire in Richard Rayner's eyes remained fierce.

Chapter Fourteen

Master Swain was a heavily built man in his early forties, with dark brown hair greying at the sides. His hardened face appeared to contain more lines than those featured on a map of London, giving testimony to vast experience in street brawling. As he pulled himself off the cobbles his face was flushed and his eyes demonstrating a burning desire to lamp this intruder who had confronted him in such an aggressive manner in his own stable yard.

Richard Rayner stepped back and waited for his grisly opponent to make his move. George Shoreditch was about to go to the Scotland Yard detective's assistance, but was stopped by Henry Bustle.

"The Inspector won't be needing our help sir," the Sergeant confirmed.

"But Swain is a strong man Sergeant and is likely to tear your Inspector to pieces."

Bustle just smiled and advised their escort to sit back and enjoy the entertainment which was to follow, advising him not to be fooled by appearances.

It soon became obvious the muscular Christopher Swain didn't adhere to the Queensberry Rules. As soon as the man had found his feet, he growled like a bear with a sore paw, throwing himself at the Inspector with both arms ready to grab Rayner and crush his ribs.

The Scotland Yard detective was slippery though and quickly stepped to one side, allowing the momentum of his opponent to carry him past, before planting a heavy fist into the back of the man's head, which resulted in another painful roar of frustration.

Swain turned and again threw himself forward with hatred in his eyes. He had every intention of inflicting serious harm to the tailor's dummy, provided he could get him in his grasp. This was proving to be a confrontation the bigger man couldn't win though, as again, he was out witted. In dealing with this attack the Inspector surprisingly fell on to his back, landing a boot into his opponent's groin, before lifting him clear of the ground and over his head. The stable manager flew through the air, landing heavily on his back. The lesson had been taught and the defeated bully lay on the cobbles severely winded, bruised and hurting.

"Please tell me you want some more of that," Rayner calmly said, standing over the man and appearing not to be even slightly breathless, whereby his opponent was wheezing in an attempt to get some air into his lungs.

"Enough I say," a voice boomed out from close by, "What in Hell's name is going on?" A small rounded man, dressed in riding britches was standing in one corner of the yard with both hands on his hips, one grasping a riding crop. Sir Neville Grimes's face was redder than the man still lying in the dirt, and his colour was accentuated by a mop of grey hair and bushy moustache to match.

George Shoreditch wasted no more time and quickly leapt from the carriage, followed by Henry Bustle.

"Sir Neville," he nervously said, "Might I introduce you to Inspector Richard Rayner and Sergeant Henry Bustle who have journeyed from Scotland Yard to assist with the Investigation into the larceny of Fleet of Foot."

The stud owner strode across the yard, before declaring, "This is a strange way to begin your Investigation Inspector, by beating up on my stable manager."

Rayner offered his hand and replied with a smile on his face, "A little exercise did no one any harm Sir Neville. I am glad to meet you at long last."

"You sound as if you have been anticipating making my acquaintance for some time sir?"

"Your son is taught by my wife at Kings College."

"Really, then it is a pleasure to welcome you Inspector." The Knight of the Realm then looked down at his stable manager who by then was sitting up, but still trying hard to breathe.

"What on earth are you doing welcoming these gentlemen from London in such an unacceptable manner Christopher?"

The man tried, but still found it difficult to speak, so Inspector George Shoreditch spoke on his behalf.

"We found your man laying a whip to one of your horse's Sir Neville, and Inspector Rayner took exception to such treatment. I'm afraid the horse ran off towards the open fields."

"Get yourself up man," the race horse owner ordered in disgust, "And go up to the house; I shall deal with you later." He then turned to Richard Rayner and offered to put up the two detectives for as long as they needed to remain.

"Please treat my home as your own Inspector," he cordially invited, "Beginning with some refreshments as soon as we leave here." He then shouted out the name of 'Robert' and a young lad seemed to appear from nowhere.

"Which mount was it?" he asked the boy.

"Rosy sir, she's at the back of the stables."

"Then go and fetch her boy, and see to her needs."

The stable boy quickly made off, but not before nodding at Richard Rayner, as if thanking him for the course of action he had just taken in cutting the lad's boss man down to size.

"If it's alright with you Sir Neville, I would like to begin my enquiries without further delay, beginning with my seeing the lad who was present when the horse was stolen."

"Of course, young Henry is out at present riding with some of the trainers and jockeys, but I expect them to return within the next hour or so."

"Then might I see the maid who prepared his supper on that dreadful night, a Miss Mavis Jennings I believe?"

"Most certainly, come I shall take you to meet the wench."

The small party of detectives then followed Sir Neville towards the impressive front of the house, where a large ornamental fountain stood in the centre of a driveway leading off in another direction away from the stable yard. The magnificent building portrayed unimaginable opulence and as they walked, Rayner whispered to Henry Bustle, instructing him to covertly stay within hearing distance of Sir Neville, once their host had left them with the maid.

The interior of the house was just as impressive as the outside, and the visitors were quickly introduced to the witness Richard Rayner had requested to see. Mavis Jennings was a slip of a girl, found working in the kitchen under the supervision of a much larger lady who was the recognised cook. Mrs Lamtree appeared to be a lady very much focused on what she was doing within her own domain.

After the initial introductions, Rayner asked if there was some where he could talk to the girl in private, and was immediately escorted to a ground floor parlour which was similar to a treasure trove of relics all connected with horse racing. As had been the case in the Graingers' house, framed paintings of various winners adorned the walls, and one glass cabinet contained a number of silver trophies awarded for various races won. Another boasted highly polished bridles and stirrups. But the most impressive item on display was placed in the centre of the shelf above the large hearth in which a fire was blazing. It was a magnificent silver cup awarded to Sir Neville Grimes for services rendered to the Jockey Club based at Epsom Race Course, according to its engraving.

Finally, after the master of the house promised that the detectives from London would not be disturbed, Rayner and Bustle were left alone with the young witness.

George Shoreditch politely asked if he could remain and his Scotland Yard counterpart agreed, watching Henry Bustle disappear out of the door in Sir Neville's footsteps.

"Now young lady," Rayner quietly addressed an extremely nervous looking Mavis Jennings, "Please be assured what you tell us from now on will be treated in the strictest confidence and you have nothing to fear."

"Yes sir," the girl whispered back, sitting upright opposite Rayner and Shoreditch who occupied a sofa.

"Firstly, could you tell us in confidence, the name of your present bo?"

The frosty apprehension of the girl was immediately swept to one side, which had been the intention behind the question. Mavis's face turned crimson as she embarrassingly sniggered, before answering, "I have no bo sir".

"I find that hard to believe Mavis; a young girl with such a pretty face must have a whole queue of young lads baying for her attention."

"No sir," she said, looking sheepishly down at the rich carpet beneath her feet and wringing her hands together.

"Well perhaps in time that will be the case. Tell me then, what do you do for recreation? Do you not have the opportunity to meet lads of your age?" Rayner was already beginning his probing stage of the interview.

"No sir, except for the monthly dance in the village. Sometimes Mrs. Lamtree lets us attend at the village hall but we have to be back by nine o'clock."

"When you say, us, who else accompanies you to those dances?"

"Only Robert and Henry, the two stable lads and we sometimes meet up with the local youths from the village."

"And I expect you are an excellent dancer Mavis? Am I correct?"

"I can twirl sir, but I'm not as good as some of the older girls who go there."

"What kind of music do they play at these shin digs?"

"There's an accordionist who plays all kinds of music sir, mostly waltzes, but my favourite is the Military Two Step."

"Ah, a lady after my own heart," Rayner claimed, sitting back with George Shoreditch wondering where his colleague's line of questioning was going.

Rayner had deliberately and successfully tried to put the girl at ease by his rapport and was ready now to delve deeper into her cognitive recollections with more poignant questions.

If Henry Bustle was exceptionally good at one thing, it was his job as a detective, and the Sergeant was standing in the hallway outside the library, having silently opened the door slightly ajar to hear the conversation within. Of course, he had already thought of a reason for him being there should any of the staff suddenly appear without warning, and continued confidently ear wigging.

Sir Neville Grimes was chastising his stable manager for having been involved in the earlier encounter with Richard Rayner and making a complete fool of himself, but from what Bustle could actually hear, the stud owner was lacking any genuine concern in his voice.

"Whilst they remain in this house, you must refrain from attracting any attention to yourself and treating any of the horses harshly. Do you understand Christopher?" Bustle overheard the owner advise, a little surprised that the suggestion appeared only to be advisable, indicating to the layman that Swain's harsh treatment of horses was acceptable to their owner.

"Now I want you to think back carefully Mavis of the times you have journeyed home from the dance."

"Yes sir."

"Can you recollect, either at any of the dances or when on your homeward journey, did you and Henry in particular ever mention taking his supper to him?" Rayner asked quietly and encouragingly.

"We always did sir. Henry was always teasing me about my ringlets and in return I always threatened to take him burnt toast for his supper, but we were only jesting with one another."

"Well done," he said, "Now think back to the man's face who offered to take Henry's supper to him. I understand you described him to Inspector Shoreditch as having fair hair and a goatee beard?"

"Yes sir."

"Where was it you last saw that man before he appeared at the kitchen door that night."

"I can't remember sir. I don't think I ever..."

"Could it have been at one of the village dances?"

The girl thought hard, until suddenly her eyes lit up and she became excited.

"He was at the dance, standing at the door just a couple of

weeks ago sir. I remember now, he smiled at me as I walked past and stepped inside."

"Was he still there when you left can you remember?"

"I don't think so, but yes, he was definitely at the dance then but he looked different somehow."

"Was he wearing different clothes?"

She nodded, again obviously remembering more and described a winged collar and tie beneath a brown checked jacket.

"But there's more sir. There was a smell about him."

"Yes Mavis, a pleasant or nasty smell? Try to remember."

The girl's eyes rolled up towards the ceiling and then she blurted out, "A pleasant smell sir. It was sweet lavender."

Richard Rayner's method of extracting every last detail from the witness had worked successfully, and after Mavis Jennings had been thanked for her assistance and invited to return to the kitchen, George Shoreditch congratulated him.

"That was a master piece of interviewing Inspector," he said with admiration, "How on earth did you know the girl had seen the man previous to the night of the larceny?"

"I didn't and you would do me a favour by calling me by my first name, Richard," Rayner answered. "It's obvious our horse thief had got to know about supper being provided by the kitchen to the stable boy responsible for watching over the steed. It was therefore highly likely he would have extracted the information from one of the kitchen staff unwittingly. If Mavis hadn't remembered having seen the man previously, then I should have used the same method when talking with the stable boy."

"How do you think it takes us further, Richard?"

"Well, we now know our man had planned his escapade very carefully and had gone to a lot of trouble in doing so, weeks prior to the actual larceny. We also know he wears a brown checked jacket with a collar and tie, denoting he is no surf. Also, George, we are now aware that he uses lavender water on his face."

Henry Bustle then entered the room and joined his two colleagues, informing Richard Rayner that a group of horses and riders had just entered the stable yard. All three then left the house and made their way back to the cobbled enclosure, where Inspector Shoreditch introduced the two visitors to the stable boy, Henry Withers, who was busy brushing down one of the horses.

Chapter Fifteen

Both Shoreditch and Bustle were surprised at what little time Richard Rayner dedicated towards questioning the stable boy. The Inspector asked but a few questions, including the time Henry Withers had finally come out of his drugged condition to find Fleet of Foot missing.

"It was early dawn sir," the lad with the unkempt mop of hair and toothy grin answered, "The sky was turning light and I immediately raised the alarm."

"Who was the first person to come to your assistance Henry?"

"Master Swain sir, and then he went up to the house to fetch the owner."

"Thank you. You must be tired after your ride so I will leave you for now and might be required to speak to you again a little later." Rayner then turned to George Shoreditch and asked the Inspector to show him how far he had managed to track the hooves of the stolen horse.

The local investigator led the way with Richard Rayner suggesting the stolen horse would most probably have had its hooves covered to avoid making any noise.

"Yes, and we noticed that from the impressions made on the grass." The local man felt that he was also in a race, with the London Inspector pushing him on, as if delay would be costly.

"What of the men who were responsible for the larceny, how many footprints did you detect alongside the horse's tracks?"

"There was only one set of footprints visible, but I take it you think there was more than one villain responsible?"

"Most definitely; the man who took the supper to young Henry would have undoubtedly had an accomplice somewhere, to assist should anything go wrong."

Shoreditch accepted the suggestion by nodding, as they headed out towards the open fields.

Although the countryside around them was fairly flat, the ground they trod was elevated and they could see for miles around them, as the late afternoon shadows began to lengthen. The trio walked for a lengthy distance, until they came to a wooden gate secured by a piece of twine looped over a fence post. George Shoreditch stopped and indicated where the hoof impressions disappeared.

"This is where I believe the horse was placed into a box and you can still see the wheel ruts of the vehicle in the lane beyond."

After passing through the gate, Rayner looked hard at the ruts in the dried mud and nodded his acquiescence, before asking, "In what general direction does this lane lead to?"

"Towards London and the North east."

"Including the County of Suffolk."

"I will take your word for that Richard. I was never any good at knowing my Geography."

Rayner stood for some time gazing in the direction suggested by his counterpart, in which the horse box appeared to have been taken with Fleet of Foot on board. He walked for a hundred yards or so, following the same wheel ruts and once again stopped, nursing his chin in deep thought.

"Yes, that must be it," he suddenly spoke aloud to no one in particular. Turning to face Henry Bustle, yet another surprise move came from the Inspector from Scotland Yard.

"Our work here is finished Henry. We shall return to London this evening," he confidently declared.

George Shoreditch looked aghast and instantly enquired, "Do you not need to make any further enquiries, such as questioning the stable boy further, and of course there is Christopher Swain who might have heard something going on when the horse was stolen?"

"I will leave those tasks to yourself George; I have every confidence in you, but we do not need any further information."

"Are you telling me you already know the identity of the thieves?"

"Yes, and please convey our regards to Sir Neville and inform him that, as far as I know, his son is doing well at Kings College. I expect to return Fleet of Foot to him in plenty of time for the horse to run in the Derby, that is of course, provided he hasn't already withdrawn him from the race."

Even Henry Bustle was mystified by Richard Rayner's unexpected decision, as the three men made their way back towards the stable yard, especially the Inspector's promise to return the horse to its rightful owner. And yet, knowing the man as he did, the Sergeant was aware he would have to patiently wait until they were alone before he could extract more information as to why there had been such a dramatic turn of events.

Having bid farewell to the local Inspector at the livery in Epsom, the Scotland Yard detectives were forced to drive their horse and carriage through the fading light of that early evening. Henry Bustle was feeling that his stomach had been cut from his throat as he complained about the lack of victuals.

"I apologise Henry," Rayner said, geeing up the horse to move more quickly along the country lanes and wanting to get back to London as soon as possible, "I was forgetting the needs of the inner man, but promise to make it up to you during the journey tomorrow. In the meantime, I am sure you would prefer to dine with your wife tonight."

"That goes without saying, but where are we off to tomorrow?"

"Why, to arrest the main culprit for the crime we have just investigated and conduct a methodical search to recover one Fleet of Foot race horse."

"Is it to be a mystery trip or am I to be informed of our destination?"

"Newmarket Henry. We shall be returning to the Grainger stud where I do believe the stolen horse is being kept concealed."

"But you believed that Sir Samuel was too much of a lover of horses to have put the animal through the kind of trauma it would have experienced in the hands of amateurs."

"Quite so, but I wasn't including his son, Roland. Cast your mind back to when we stood in the library at Sir Samuel's house, can you recall a scent which was easily detectable?"

"I can only recall the grandeur of the whole house."

"Lavender Henry, it was quite a distinctive odour inside that library, and I made one important mistake by not interviewing Sir Samuel's son and daughter in law, Emily Wake. The thief back at Sir Neville Grimes's stables wore lavender water and I suspect when we see Roland Grimes, he will answer the description given to us by a very reliable Mavis Jennings."

It was very late by the time Richard Rayner dropped his Sergeant off at his home in Lambeth, before finally returning to his own domicile in Richmond. When arriving at his final destination the Inspector was feeling extremely tired and worn out. Being convinced his theory was both factual and provable, Rayner enthusiastically believed a return journey to Cheveley village would be fruitful. But, both himself and Henry Bustle needed to be fresh in undertaking such a task, so had arranged to meet at the later time of ten o'clock the following morning. However, a sleepless night followed, with his thoughts refusing to stop constantly churning over every small detail of what they had discovered so far.

The eventual discovery of those responsible for the larceny of the horse taken from Epsom hadn't really been difficult for an investigator possessing the kind of skills with which Rayner was blessed. But in trying to seek out a link between that crime and the murders which had taken place, was a different matter altogether. He lay awake with a sleeping Clarice at his side, trying hard to come to terms with that particular paradox. Rayner felt they were missing something which could easily have been staring them in the face, but what was it exactly? When morning came, the Inspector was still struggling with the problem.

It was mid-afternoon when the detectives rode into Sir Samuel Grainger's
stable yard and were met by the stable manager, Jack Lashley.

"You have some news for Sir Samuel then?" the man enquired.

"No, not as yet, but you might have Master Lashley," Rayner answered, "I wish to intrude upon your local knowledge sir, if that is agreeable?"

"Of course Inspector, any way in which I can be of assistance."

"I am looking for a disused building or large shed nearby; a stable would be preferable, somewhere which is located in a position rarely visited."

Jack Lashley thought for some time before acknowledging that there were several old farm buildings in the vicinity which were no longer in use and located in isolated positions.

"Can you furnish me with more details?" he asked.

"Only to tell you that the enclosure has to be big enough to stable a horse."

"That doesn't help much, as any of those I have in mind are of that size, but most of them are dilapidated and haven't been used for a long time."

"Then might I suggest we start at the disused building closest to this yard."

Jack Lashley looked confused, but quickly suggested they should begin their search on horseback rather than in the visitors' carriage.

"An excellent idea, can you arrange that for us."

"Wait here for one jiff; I take it you can both ride?"

"Yes, but Henry here might benefit from a more docile mount if one is available."

The man nodded before disappearing into one of the enclosures.

"Do we really have to go on horseback?" an anxious Henry Bustle asked, obviously perturbed by the thought of spending some time in the saddle.

"The terrain we are likely to cover Henry warrants such transport. Be brave,

we won't exactly be racing around."

"I just hope that Sir Neville Grimes will fully appreciate the trouble we are going to in order to recover his nag."

"Think of the horse being a treasure chest filled to the gunnels with all kinds of gold bangles and rare gems, for that's what she is."

"And there was me thinking it was just a four-legged beast."

Rayner smiled and turned to see Jack Lashley reappearing with the reins of two thoroughbreds in his grasp and the stable boy Nicholas leading a third. He indicated the horse which the Sergeant should mount and within a few minutes all three left the yard with the stable manager showing the way.

The Inspector could see from a distance that the first structure they visited wouldn't be suitable, having half its roof caved in, so they continued to the next, and then the next, until their guide had to admit they were running out of possible locations. Finally, he stopped and turned to Rayner, suggesting that to view other likely buildings they would have to go further afield and outside his local knowledge.

"Very well," the Inspector said, "Perhaps I need to come at this from a different angle altogether, but thank you for trying for us."

When all three returned to the stable yard, Richard Rayner immediately climbed the incline towards the main house, where they had previously visited, with a very sore Henry Bustle walking a lot slower behind him.

"Keep walking Henry," the senior detective suggested, referring to the aching in Bustle's buttocks, "It will soon wear off with exercise."

"I doubt that very much," the wincing Sergeant called back.

They were allowed inside by the butler and asked if they could speak with Roland Grainger, the owner's son.

"I'm afraid he's not here sir," the butler explained, "Master Roland has gone with his father to Newmarket and is not expected to return until much later. Shall I inform Lady Grainger of your return?"

"No, there is no need, but perhaps you could invite Mrs. Emily Grainger to join us in the library please?"

The butler bowed and disappeared, leaving both detectives to find their own way into the library. There it was again, the same aroma which had lingered in the room during their last visit. The Sergeant however was unable to smell it, even after the Inspector described it as being lavender.

"You really do need to get that crooked nose of yours straightened out Henry," Rayner suggested."

It seemed to take an age before someone opened the door and stepped inside the room to join the visitors. Emily Grainger was a slightly built young lady with fair hair pinned up on top of her head, and Richard Rayner could see a resemblance to her brother, Thomas Wake. Although attractive, she also looked somewhat nervous and was immediately invited to take a seat by the Inspector. The first thing the Inspector did was to ensure the young lady was not wearing the same perfume which had invaded the library. She wasn't.

"It's your husband we have really come to see, but I'm confident you will be able to help us recover the horse taken from Sir Neville Grimes stables," he said, interested in the kind of response he would get from the lady.

"How could anyone from here help you do that Inspector?" she answered insincerely.

"Oh, I do believe earnestly that you can Mrs. Grainger. When are you expecting your husband home?"

"Later this evening, he's gone to Newmarket with Sir Samuel."

"Therefore, we cannot wait any longer. We need to get Fleet of Foot back to its rightful owner as quickly as possible, and I am relying on your co-operation in taking us to where the filly is hidden."

"But how can I possibly assist you?" She was having problems looking at either Richard Rayner or Henry Bustle directly, and the Inspector noticed how the lady's delicate hands were uncontrollably trembling.

"Because you and your husband took it from the stables in Epson," Rayner alleged, standing from his seat and towering over the woman, "I want you to listen very carefully to what I am about to say Mrs. Grainger. At the moment, as far as we are concerned, the horse is missing and if we can return her fairly soon, I am confident I can persuade Sir Neville not to press for any prosecution. But we need to find out where she is urgently."

Emily Grainger sat there, speechless for a time, staring into the fire and obviously giving a great deal of thought to what Rayner had said.

The Inspector then whispered to her, "The game is up I'm afraid, why else do you think we are here?"

She then looked up at him and quietly asked, "How am I guaranteed I will not be prosecuted?"

"You are not madam, but I believe that will be the case if the horse is returned and is able to run in the Derby, which is a few weeks away yet."

"What you seek is being looked after by a neighbour of ours who also runs his own stud, but doesn't know the true identity of the horse."

"And what is the name of this kind neighbour?"

"Graham and Violet Parkes have a small business over in Moulton, but they believe that Fleet of Foot is one of our horses and are temporarily looking after her in the belief we do not have the room."

"Describe your husband to us Mrs. Grainger," Rayner then requested.

"He had nothing to do with any of this Inspector."

"I believe he did. How could you possibly have taken that horse on your own and we already know a man was involved in drugging one of the stable boys."

"I have admitted responsibility, is that not sufficient?"

Unknown to either detective, their conversation with Emily Grainger was being listened to from the other side of the library's closed door. Neither did they see Lady Grainger riding at a gallop away from the stables, heading in the direction of Newmarket.

Chapter Sixteen

Emily Grainger found herself in a hopeless position with no one to turn to, except the two men who had unravelled details of her secret, and the role she had played in the theft of the race horse. After deliberating for a short while on her precarious position, she decided the only option she had was to place her trust in Richard Rayner. Was the Inspector a man of his word? Would she avoid incarceration by co-operating fully with the detectives? Only time would answer those questions.

The lady reluctantly accompanied the men from Scotland Yard across the open countryside, having been invited to travel in their carriage. When they approached the hamlet of Moulton, a guilt-ridden Emily pointed them in the direction of the stables owned by Graham and Violet Parkes.

The yard was, as expected, a great deal smaller than that

which they had left with just ten stalls contained within its perimeter. As soon as the carriage came to a halt, their guide jumped down and approached one enclosure at the far end. She then stood stroking the nose of a chestnut filly which had its head protruding from one of the stalls.

"This is the horse you have been searching for Inspector," she confirmed.

A young woman with a far more robust appearance than her friend from the Grainger stud, could be seen walking towards the visitors having come from a small detached cottage situated at the back of the stables.

"Good afternoon Emily my dear, have you come to take her home now," Violet Parkes pleasantly enquired. She was proudly wearing a man's large soft cap and what appeared to be an oversized ankle length brown cow gown.

"Yes Violet, these gentlemen have come to help me."

Both detectives nodded to the lady who immediately entered the stall, proclaiming in a husky voice, the filly had already been fed and watered, and required a bridle.

Within a few minutes the horse had been tethered to the back of the carriage and Richard Rayner slowly and carefully drove it back towards the Grainger's residence.

"At first Inspector it was meant to be a prank, but when we heard that Scotland Yard had been called in to investigate, we, that is I, became worried that perhaps I had gone too far."

"Why did you take the horse in the first place?" Henry Bustle asked, already thinking he knew the answer.

"To teach that braggard, Grimes a lesson. Over recent weeks the man has been tormenting my father in law about which horse would win the Derby, often referring to our horse, Green Eyes, as an old nag which would be left at the starting post."

"Well you did that alright," Bustle confirmed, "He's been out of his mind believing he wouldn't have a runner in the race."

She turned to Richard Rayner and enquired, "What will happen to me now Inspector. Will I have to go back to London with you?" It was a plea for mercy rather than a question.

"Not just yet, but I do believe we should discuss your position with both your husband and Sir Samuel. I fear we shall be requiring the loan of a horse box in which to transport Fleet of Foot back to its rightful owner. But I do have one question for you. Were you involved in the doping of the stable boy on the night the horse was taken?"

"I know nothing about that sir," she lied.

When they returned to the Grainger stables, Rayner told

Bustle to wait with Fleet of Foot, before following the young lady up to the house, where they were met by an extremely anxious looking Sir and Lady Grainger, both looking extremely concerned.

"My word Emily, what has happened?" the mistress of the house enquired, throwing a look of scornful disdain at the Inspector.

Rayner answered on behalf of their daughter in law, but ignored the woman who had asked the question and addressed his answer to Sir Samuel Grainger. He explained what had taken place and that with some help from the man's daughter in law, they had recovered the stolen horse.

Sir Samuel looked utterly disgusted, but still managed to ask the man from Scotland Yard what would happen to Emily, the mother of his two grandchildren.

"She can explain that to you later sir," Rayner suggested, "But what is more urgent is that I speak with your son, Roland."

"I'm afraid that is not possible Inspector, I left him to continue with our business affairs at Newmarket where he will be staying the night."

"I see, and now that he is fully aware of our interest in him, will he be returning in the morning or has he decided to take a holiday on the continent?" the Inspector accused, guessing that both Roland Grainger and his father would have been tipped off about the detectives' presence. Rayner also suspected that his quarry hadn't the backbone to face his responsibilities and would remain in hiding like a sewer rat for the time being, until his wife's plight had become known.

"I resent that notion sir," the fugitive's father announced, putting the Inspector immediately on the front foot.

"You can resent it all you wish Sir Samuel, that is your prerogative, but I speak only of facts." Rayner considered arresting Emily Grainger and holding her in custody back in London, until her husband had surrendered himself for interrogation. However, having declared otherwise to the woman, he felt obliged to keep to his promise. The young lady had put her trust in him and Rayner was a man of his word.

"I do believe, considering all that has happened," he continued, "The least you can do sir, is provide adequate transport in which to return Fleet of Foot back to its owner."

At first the race horse owner coloured up and glared back at Rayner, but then succumbed to his request.

"You can borrow one of the horse boxes and I shall provide a stable boy to follow you with the damned horse inside."

"Thank you. I shall explain to Sir Neville Grimes that you sir had nothing to do with the abduction of his horse, and that you genuinely regret what has taken place. I suspect such an act of contrition might well persuade the man not to take any further action. Having said that, this escapade was carefully planned by your son, and it did involve an innocent stable boy being doped whilst the so-called prank took place."

"God damn him," the Knight of the Realm exclaimed, before quickly recomposing himself and offering to pay some form of monetary compensation to his competitor for the inconvenience his son had caused.

"As much as I detest the man," he said, referring to Sir Neville, "I also deplore the actions of my son and daughter in law. I shall be forever in your debt though Inspector if you can help us avoid any future prosecution."

"I shall do my utmost sir. How much in compensation are you willing to pay and what amount can I can offer to Sir Neville on your behalf?"

"A hundred guineas, but only because of the harm which might have been caused to the stable boy."

"A generous offer sir, now if we can arrange for Fleet of Foot to be stabled for tonight. we shall be on our way at first light in the morning."

"Then I shall have rooms prepared for you," Sir Samuel offered, looking towards his wife.

"That won't be necessary sir, we shall take rooms in the village and return first thing. I take it I can trust you to ensure Fleet of Foot is cared for overnight by yourself personally?"

The race horse owner hesitated, before swearing his oath the horse would be kept safe and secured under his personal supervision.

"And your word sir that nothing untoward will happen to the filly."

"You have my word Inspector. I am not in the habit of doping horses, unlike Sir Neville Grimes."

"I shall telegram you with Sir Neville's decision but whatever the outcome is I must emphasise my disappointment at the behaviour of your son."

"You can rest assured Inspector, Roland will pay in full for his unacceptable misdemeanour."

Rayner nodded, before leaving to re-join Henry Bustle. He was well aware he could later face criticism of what could be regarded as having taken a lenient course of action. Nevertheless, the Inspector had only become involved in this particular felony as a result of the Inquiry into much graver crimes.

The following morning, after leaving the Peacock Inn in Cheveley, both detectives arrived in the stable yard just as the first signs of daylight were appearing in the eastern sky. They found the stable boy Nicholas waiting for them, having already moved Fleet of Foot into a box.

"I shall follow you sir," the lad confirmed.

"Very well Nicholas, we shall travel steady and I hope to be at the Grimes's stud about lunch time."

On their way north, they skirted around London, moving more slowly than anticipated, and Henry Bustle wasted few words in describing how he felt about having apparently let Roland Grainger off the hook.

"It seems to me he was the main instigator of this whole torrid affair Inspector and the man had despicably left his wife to take the consequences."

"Perhaps Henry, but without turning this affair into something much bigger, I think we've taken the right course of action and trust his father will deal with him severely."

"I would deal with him severely by cutting off his bollocks, sir."

"Your far from judicious way with words Henry, forever amazes me."

By the time both the carriage and horse box finally arrived at the Epsom stud if was mid-afternoon, and as if Sir Neville Grimes was uncannily expecting their arrival, they found him standing in the yard. He appeared to be examining one of his horse's in the company of his stable manager, the over aggressive Christopher Swain. When he saw the two detectives and the horse box following behind, a look of optimism immediately swept across his weathered face.

"You've found her Inspector," he called out, more in hope.

"Yes sir, she's in the horse box and appears to be in good health."

Fleet of Foot was quickly taken from the transport and led to a stable by Swain, who seemed to be scrutinising every physical part of the horse as she walked alongside him.

"Fancy trusting that bullying excuse for a man with such a valuable horse," Bustle murmured under his breath.

"Perhaps we could retire to your house Sir Neville and I will explain everything to you," Rayner suggested, ignoring his Sergeant's adverse comment, "But first perhaps arrangements could be made for young Nicholas to rest over night before returning with the horsebox in the morning."

"Where's the boy from?" Sir Neville asked.

"He's one of Sir Samuel Grainger's stable boys." Rayner then went on to describe the course of events as the two men walked up towards the house, with Henry Bustle following. He omitted to mention Roland Grainger's involvement by design, not wishing to fuel the victim's anger further. By the time the Inspector had finished reiterating his explanations, they had reached the library and the master of the house was pouring out three celebratory tumblers of brandy for himself and his two successful visitors.

"Words fail me Inspector," he finally said, "And a foolish prank you say by that snobbish prat's daughter in law."

"Yes, but Sir Samuel was not involved and leant us the horse box in which we could safely return Fleet of Foot. He also offers to pay you compensation for your inconvenience along with his deepest apologies for what has taken place."

"How much compensation?"

"One hundred guineas in return for a promise not to take the matter further."

"Well now, that's a guilty man for you, but I'm not one to hold a grudge, particularly as we now have our future Derby winner back in the fold, provided of course he parts with his money without delay."

"I shall let him know of your acceptance of his offer as soon as possible, and in the meantime, I suggest you tighten your security arrangements in future."

Sir Neville looked affronted by Rayner's suggestion, but allowed it to pass by without offering any comment.

When returning to London later that same afternoon, their first visit was to a telegram office to send confirmation of Sir Neville's acceptance of compensation to Sir Samuel Grainger. Scotland Yard then beckoned, where Rayner intended updating the Superintendent on what had taken place.

They found Frederick Morgan sitting in his smoke free office and the Head of the Detective Branch was quite satisfied with the outcome of the stolen horse inquiry. He expressed however, disappointment that no one would be arraigned for the offence, but decided to leave it to his Inspector's judgement.

"So, Rayner, when do you intend returning to a small matter of three murders?"

"We have never left it sir, there is still much to do, but I am confident we are on the verge of success."

"Has there been another murder whilst we have been away sir?" Henry Bustle enquired.

"Do you think I would still be sitting here if there had been?"

the Superintendent snapped back, "Isn't three enough for you?"

"Yes of course sir, but I was just wondering…"

"You're not paid to wonder Bustle. Leave that to your betters."

"I was wondering if that baker you arrested sir was worthy of further investigation," the Sergeant dared to suggest, bringing Morgan's facial colouring up to a more intense level.

It was time to leave, before an imminent explosion of fury wrapped itself around the Sergeant, who had been out of order in Rayner's view. Quickly the Inspector left to return to his own office, with Henry Bustle at his side.

"At times Henry, you go too far," Rayner commented in chastisement.

"It's just that the Superintendent's supercilious attitude riles me so much," the Sergeant replied.

"I think we have earned an early night," the Inspector suggested, much to his Sergeant's delight, "So let us away to our homes and catch up on some much-needed rest. I shall meet you at the Riverside Café in the morning for breakfast and we can then focus our minds back on the atrocities linked to the workhouses."

Bustle had every intention of following the Inspector's advice, but not before visiting the front desk downstairs to enquire whether any additional reports had been received of commercial horses having gone missing. Much to his surprise and amazement, the desk sergeant informed him that in total there had been twenty of the four legged animals reported stolen from all over London, since the epidemic of rustling had begun. Henry Bustle would not be going directly home on that particular evening.

Chapter Seventeen

From all the informants Henry Bustle had cultivated during his time as a detective, Fat Annie had been the most productive. The woman lived in one of the upper tiered rooms of a dingy courtyard in Whitechapel, with a railed balustrade running around its perimeter accessing the many tiny slum residences. She was a huge woman with breasts the size of melons and three chins supporting a pale face sufficiently ugly to be deemed scary. Annie knew just about everybody and their business in that part of the East End, and was virtually a permanent fixture sitting outside her door. If there had ever been a Daily Bugle for distributing snippets of gossip around the East End, it was Fat Annie.

As soon as the Sergeant appeared within the courtyard below, the rotund lady's voice boomed out for every neighbour to hear.

"Come for a free one 'ave you 'Enery?"

There was a time when the big woman's taunts used to embarrass him, but not now. The information she could usually provide was worth being the object of derision and jibe. Bustle looked up and doffed his bowler at the mass of human flesh looking over the top of the balustrade at him, before making for the far corner where steps leading to the upper level could be found.

As he scaled the steps to reach the balcony, the Sergeant could sense a hundred pairs of eyes watching him from behind drab curtains, having heard one or two doors slammed shut. When he finally came face to face with the grotesque woman, she straightened her back and thrust out her breasts in front of him.

"A tanner's worth is the usual price 'Enery, but as you're a regular you can have a fondle luvvie for a penny for each of 'em." She then laughed out loud, as if a clap of thunder had just descended on the surrounding hovels.

Without saying another word, the woman turned and entered her own small domain with Bustle following her, as if he was just another desperate customer seeking the lady's abominable services. Once inside, the door was closed and the Sergeant immediately produced a small glass bottle containing 'women's ruin' – gin. Without speaking a word, the gift was opened in haste and introduced to the gaping hole she called a mouth. Then after taking a long gulp, Fat Annie smiled and in a quieter voice jokingly suggested the Sergeant's business must have been important, seeing as he'd called on her when it was still light outside.

"There's been a spate of horses being parted from their owners Annie. Any ideas?"

"Perhaps it's those tax collecting bastards taking what's owed them in kind," she jested, "How do yer think I pay mine 'Enery?"

"I'm serious, there's been twenty gee gees disappeared in a matter of a few weeks."

"Want a cuppa luvvie, or would you prefer to join me in slinging the contents of this bottle you've brought me down my gullet?" The lady had a way with words and for people other than the likes of Henry Bustle, would require a translator.

"Tea would be fine duckie," he confessed, never refusing the offer of refreshments whereby the person offering might be offended by a refusal to participate in their particular flea infested domain.

He watched as the grotesque mass waddled over to a grease covered gas stove standing in one corner of the room, before striking a light beneath a tin kettle which had seen far better days.

"Hosses you say?" she asked, turning to face him once again.

"Twenty of them."

"It's the Micks that lives in the 'Holy Land'," she suggested, referring to the most denigrated part of Whitechapel known as the Rookery, a haven for mostly Irish migrants.

"'Enery, I've seen the smarmy bastards with my own eyes shifting two or three hosses down towards the river. If any of your brainless peelers had opened their eyes, they'd have seen them loading up a ferry which takes them around the coast and across to Ireland."

"To sell them off over there I suppose? They must have a market for so much horse flesh."

"Christ 'Enery, who's the blue bottle here? Can't you fathom it out yerself? It's a profitable business luvvie getting them to their own country before then shipping them out to the continent to sell as meat to them foreign butchers."

"Horse meat," he remarked, chastising himself for not having thought of that.

"Well they wouldn't be sold on as Squirrel meat now would they. Them foreigners have a liking for a few juicy steaks of hoss meat, I can tell yer."

"Do you know who's behind it?"

"Now that kind of information costs hard cash my Scotland Yard ferret."

"There's a fiver back at the Yard waiting to be paid for such intelligence."

"A tenner 'Enery and not a penny less luvvie."

"God Almighty Annie, you drive a hard bargain, but you'll get it, if it's worth that much."

The steaming hot water was poured into the crock teapot, before the infamous and popular woman volunteered, "Two brothers; Michael and Flinty Gallagher, or at least I knows they're both involved. Whether they are just labourers or not I don't rightly knows, but I can't see the Gallaghers working for anybody else except themselves."

"Any idea where this ferry ties up on the river?"

"At Blackfriars, just down from the bridge."

"That's some distance to drive horses along without being seen Annie?"

"Not in the middle of the night it ain't." The contents of the tea pot were then poured into an old cracked cup and handed over to the Sergeant who nodded in appreciation. There was no milk because she couldn't afford any, except on special occasions, and this wasn't one of them.

"Any idea where these Gallagher brothers live in the Holy Land?"

"No I ain't but it won't take you long to sort them out. One's big and noisy with a gob on him like a ship's funnel. That's Michael and his brother is like a strip of piss with little to say for himself at the best of times; that's Flinty. You'll most probably find the pair of them in The Quartermaster in Great Russell Street most nights."

Bustle finished drinking his tea and thanked the lady for her help, before turning to open the door.

"Don't forget my twenty quid 'Enery," she said.

"If you mean the tenner I promised Annie, I've never let you down yet have I?"

The woman chuckled as her visitor stepped through the doorway.

After leaving the cluster of small hovels, the Sergeant headed for Westminster Bridge, which would take him across the river to Lambeth where he lived. His visit to his informant had been well worthwhile, but somehow, he had to convince Richard Rayner it was necessary to put a stop to such deplorable crimes. They needed to capture Michael and Flinty Gallagher quickly, before other hardworking men were put out of business.

Before attending at the Riverside Café to meet his Detective Sergeant for breakfast, the Inspector called at Scotland Yard early to speak with Jack Robinson. He found the young Sergeant in the basement scrutinising a number of folders containing various records. The seconded man was invited to accompany Rayner to the pre-arranged meeting with Bustle, and as they walked towards the river, described how far he had got with the enquiry into the three individual workhouses.

"I've managed to whittle the list down to five children who, twenty years ago went to both the Christchurch and Cannon Street Workhouses at the same time as Conal Gumbley and Elias Thompson were Administrators at each of them respectively."

"From that five, how many also attended at Upper Clapton at the same time as Claude Grimbold was the manager?"

"None at present, but I'm still searching through those records sir."

Rayner then called at a telegram office to send a communication to Inspector George Shoreditch at Epsom, to inform him of the conclusion of his Inquiry. The local man deserved that courtesy.

When they arrived at the café, they found Henry Bustle already sitting on an outside balcony overlooking the River

Thames, with a pot of tea in front of him. Rayner had suggested previously that his colleague should have been a polar bear, never appearing to be bothered by cold weather or chilly breezes.

"I haven't ordered breakfast yet," the cold bloodied man declared, "Thinking it would be better to wait for you to turn up first."

"Thank you, Henry, so let's get on with it. I am absolutely famished," Rayner said, calling over a waiter.

After placing their orders, the senior Sergeant related details of his previous evening's visit to Whitechapel, outlining what Fat Annie had told him about the two Gallagher brothers taking horses to be ferried across to Ireland, and then the continent to be butchered and sold as meat.

Rayner sat and listened with interest until Bustle had finished.

"What do you propose we do Sergeant?" he asked, "Pass your information on to one of the other detectives to take some action?"

"I'd rather not sir," the Sergeant replied.

His Inspector appreciated that Bustle had become more than a little interested in the wave of horse stealing incidents which had been taking place. He would be devastated if he now had to leave any future enquiries with another officer.

The breakfasts were served, which gave Rayner the opportunity to consider Bustle's position more, as he tucked into the food together with his two colleagues. After a short lapse of time he then asked the senior Sergeant, "I take it we have no name of this ferry that's manoeuvring up and down the Thames?"

"No sir, only that it docks at night just up from Blackfriars."

"Very well Henry, then seek the assistance of the River Police to keep an eye out and to contact us should they sight such a non-descript vessel near to where you say the horses are being loaded."

A broad grin suddenly appeared on Bustle's face and he told the Inspector he would get on to it straight away.

"Now gentlemen, let us get down to the business of our main Investigation." Rayner continued, reminding the other two of what they had learned so far.

"Are you still convinced that gambling at horse race meetings is the common denominator with all three murders?" Bustle asked.

"Yes, but I'm not quite sure in what form that takes, linking each of the victims."

"It might be worthwhile Inspector checking out the bookmakers working on the various race courses to see if any had dealings with any of our victims," Jack Robinson suggested.

"That's an excellent idea Jack, but I think we should shelve such a notion until a time comes when we run out of ideas, only because such a venture could take months to cover every book maker in the country."

"And what if we find one bookmaker who has dealt with all three victims in the past, what would that prove?" a pessimistic Henry Bustle asked.

"Whether or not they were in such heavy debt they became the subject of murder," Robinson suggested further, impressing the Inspector with his analytical way of thinking.

"Henry, I have a specific task for you which I think you will find interesting. I need you to look into the background of our friend, Roland Grainger, and confirm for us whether the man is really the son of Sir Samuel. Although he featured in that bizarre incident involving his wife, we don't know that much about him, only what we have been told by others. I suggest your starting point should be the Parish records covering Cheveley."

Bustle nodded.

"In the meantime, I intend visiting an acquaintance who knows the intricacies of horse racing like the back of his hand."

"Lord Dear?"

"Yes, you've heard me mention his name before. I believe he's retired now as a race horse owner but what he doesn't know about the sport isn't worth mentioning."

"Will you be taking Mrs. Rayner with you sir?" Henry Bustle asked.

"What a splendid idea Henry. I might just do that."

"I thought you might."

Clarice was thrilled when she first thought she would be going for a ride out into the countryside with her husband to visit a Peer of the Realm. But the lady's enthusiasm quickly disappeared when Richard Rayner explained he would meet Lord Dear at the Palace of Westminster. They mutually agreed it might therefore be better if she wasn't to take more time away from her work.

"By the way Richard," she said, "James Cleaver, a former alchemist and now a research lecturer at work has looked at those labels for you." She produced the three items and handed them back to her husband.

"Was he able to identify what that brown stain on the labels was?"

"Yes, James told me it contained elements of menthol and a substance known as," she paused to consult a small note pad at her side before continuing, "Chloroxylenol, a disinfectant used for cleaning the skin."

"Did he have an opinion as to where such an embrocation could be found?"

"Oh yes, virtually anywhere. According to James, menthol and chloroxylenol are the basic ingredients of horse liniment."

Rayner sat forward to the edge of his seat and his wife immediately noticed the look of interest on his face.

"Be wary though Richard," she continued, still referring to her note pad, "Apparently, when diluted it can be used by humans."

"If that was the case here Clarice, it would be one hell of a coincidence."

Chapter Eighteen

The lithe, scruffy figure of a man skipped through the heavy rain as it fell with some force, bouncing off the pavements and driving most of the populace off the streets. He stopped where he could shelter in an enclosed alleyway with his rat like features concentrating on the opposite side of the narrow street. In his eyeline he gazed upon a horse and cart waiting patiently outside a hardware shop. The vehicle had the name of 'Thomas Cartwright Haulers' painted on the sides. The owner was indeed busy inside the shop, concluding that day's delivery of sacks containing nuts and bolts with the proprietor.

Just as Master Cartwright was about to say his farewell to the local tradesman, another entered the shop. He was a huge man with close knit curly hair, a full beard and an ear ring attached to one of his lobes.

"Ah, I see I've won my bet," said the stranger in a broad Irish accent, addressing the owner of the horse and cart.

The hauler looked at him and asked bluntly, "What wager would that be then?"

"That you resembled a frog with a straw stuck up its arse having been blown up out of all proportion."

"Why you insolent bastard, I've a good mind to box your ears."

At that the shop owner called out, enquiring as to the reason why the Irishman was picking a fight with his deliveryman.

"In the name of the Virgin Mary and all that's good, I wouldn't be picking a fight where the odds are so heavily stacked against my opponent," the aggressor claimed, watching as Thomas Cartwright, who looked as though he could handle himself, raised both fists.

Whilst the planned altercation was going on inside the Hardware shop, the diminutive figure outside was busy putting his knife to good use, by cutting through the leather straps which helped to secure the horse in between the cart's shoulders. He worked speedily until the horse was free of its restriction and then casually led the animal away and out of sight.

Not one blow was struck inside the shop and the Irishman continued with a stream of insults until, satisfied he had held the victim's attention for long enough. Doffing his cloth cap to the bemused shop keeper and hauler, the Irishman quickly turned and disappeared out through the door.

"Now would you believe that aggravating bog trotter Tommy?" the shop keeper remarked.

When Thomas Cartwright finally returned to the street, he found his cart leaning forward on it shoulders with the horse nowhere to be seen. Then he realised what all the fuss had been about inside the Hardware shop. Another report was quickly made to Scotland Yard by an outraged local businessman, and Henry Bustle was informed immediately, having requested that was the first course of action to be taken.

Richard Rayner and just about everyone else inside the house was awakened by the loud banging on the front door. His pocket watch told him the time was well past one o'clock in the morning. Having a good idea what the reason was for the constable to be standing in the driveway at the front of his house, the Inspector hastily got dressed.

"Sorry sir," the officer apologised, "But Sergeant Bustle has instructed me to take you to William Street near to Blackfriars Bridge as soon as possible."

With Rayner sitting safely secured inside the carriage, trying to shake off the effects of a deep sleep, the transport galloped across London until reaching its destination. There was another horse and carriage parked in William Street, in complete darkness and containing four constables.

As soon as the Inspector had stepped down on to the wet pavement, an invigorated Henry Bustle appeared from the shadows. He quickly and quietly explained that the River Police were surreptitiously watching a ferry which was tied up a little down river, showing no lights,

"Have you seen it Henry?"

"Yes sir, I have a man watching it as we speak."

"Then let's get down there."

The Sergeant quietly summoned the small group of constables he had brought with him, and the party of law enforcers quickly made their way down from Blackfriars Bridge until the suspect vessel came into view. Each and every one of them was then quietly deployed into covert positions close to the ferry, before both the two detectives found their own concealed observations point from which they could see the whole length of the boat.

"How long has it been here, do we know?" Rayner quietly asked.

"About half an hour now sir."

"Then I shouldn't think we shall have to wait too long Henry."

As the Inspector spoke the sound of horses' hooves striking the cobbles reached them from close by.

Soon afterwards the two Gallagher brothers came into view, each leading a dray horse. As they approached, two men on the ferry also appeared from the darkness and could be seen to place a wide boarding plank from the vessel on to the short pier. Patience was the key and both detectives waited and watched with the Sergeant grasping a whistle in one hand, and a large heavy club in the other.

They continued observing as the horses were led on to the access board before being coerced into the back of the vessel. Just as one of the brothers was being handed a wad of notes by one of the bargees, Rayner nodded at his colleague.

Within seconds of Henry Bustle blowing on his whistle, constables were boarding the ferry and the two Gallagher brothers leapt from the vessel back to shore, before taking off in different directions.

The Sergeant ran after the heaviest of the couple, leaving Rayner to capture the rat faced weasel, whose spindly legs were carrying him back towards Blackfriars Bridge as fast as they could move.

Michael Gallagher's flight lasted just a couple of hundred yards before the Irishman turned and produced an iron crow bar, standing to face his pursuer menacingly, and with a grin across his bearded face. No words were spoken and as the fugitive struck out with the weapon, Bustle felt it scrape across his back as he dived forward and grabbed his man around the waist forcing him down to the ground. The crow bar went flying from the Irish man's hand and the Sergeant sat astride him, pummelling his face with his fists.

Gallagher was a strong man though and fought back, spitting and trying hard to gouge out his opponent's eyes. Then Bustle's truncheon came into play and he began clobbering his man across the head until he felt the strength of the Irishman ebb away.

"For fucks sake man, enough," Michael Gallagher pleaded.

The Sergeant then turned him over on to his stomach, and pinioned both of the man's muscular arms around his back, before securing his wrists with handcuffs.

Richard Rayner's confrontation with the man he was chasing ended in a lot less violence than his colleague had to deal with.

Upon reaching a point below the rail lines which ran parallel to Blackfriars Bridge, Flinty Gallagher had tripped and gone flying, banging his head against a stanchion. When the Inspector reached him the horse thief was still dazed, crouching down and holding his head in both hands.

Rayner cuffed him, before leading him back to where the ferry had been secured by the constables. A River Police launch was positioned across its bow. In fact, the Sergeant in charge of the launch offered to take the four prisoners back to Wapping where the River Police were based and Rayner agreed. The Scotland Yard men accepted responsibility for transporting the two stolen horses, one of which belonged to Thomas Cartwright, to the Royal Mews for stabling, until their owners could be identified and asked to collect them.

It had been a successful operation and Henry Bustle was overjoyed.

"You've done well Henry," Richard Rayner said, congratulating his Sergeant.

"Thank you, sir, I'm just relieved we've managed to put a stop to this."

"One of these days we're actually going to get back to investigating three murders which require our attention."

"I know sir, but it's just that I cannot bear hearing about dumb animals being unnecessarily stolen and butchered just to fill the purses of despicable rogues such as those two, and the couple on the boat."

"I agree Henry, but I'm off back to bed now whilst there is still time to catch up on some sleep. I'll leave this with you. I suspect you might have to arrange for those horses to be walked across to the mews." At that, the Detective Inspector turned and walked away, heading for his carriage and a warm bed.

Lord Dear was a tall distinctive looking man with short grey hair and fashionable mutton chop whiskers. He was an imposing figure, immaculately attired in a black coat with tails over a silver satin cravat, which was secured by a ruby pin beneath a fawn vest. Richard Rayner had been fortunate, having decided to visit the Palace of Westminster first in search of the peer, and having found his quarry sitting taking refreshments in the vastness of the Royal Gallery.

His Lordship's son, Rupert, had studied at Oxford the same time as the Inspector, and Rayner had met the young man's father on several occasions when visiting the family home outside Stratford upon Avon. At the time, the Peer of the Realm owned a fairly successful race horse stud from which a string of major winners was produced. That was before Sir Bartholomew Dear, as he was known then, finally retired following his call to the peerage. Most of his time in retirement from horse racing had been spent manoeuvring in and out of Parliamentary affairs.

The quietly spoken gentleman stood and smiled when he first saw Richard Rayner approaching and warmly welcomed him with a genuine firm handshake.

"My word Richard," he proclaimed, "I have read so much about your exploits I feel as though I am in the company of a celebrity."

Rayner looked embarrassed and quickly played down his public recognition and image. After accepting an invitation to take tea with his Lordship, both men settled into the soft red leather chairs provided. Their orders were placed with one of the many waitresses who constantly remained close by to assist when required.

"So, what brings you into my world young man?" Lord Dear enquired.

The Inspector shared every detail of his current Investigation, placing some emphasis on the dilemma he faced in trying to connect all three victims with attending race meetings.

"I was hoping My Lord that from your vast experience with the sport, you might just come up with some plausible notion or explanation to confirm the mutual interest of our victims was no coincidence?" he finally confirmed.

His Lordship sat back, relaxed and giving serious consideration to the interesting challenge now confronting him.

"Of course," he said quietly, "It could be that the three men you speak of are not connected in any way with each other, and it could be coincidental each of them had been a keen racegoer."

"I have thought of that My Lord, but my suspicions of some commonalty existing between them is based on a number of coincidences, which I refuse to accept have no meaning. I am now convinced their killer comes from the horse racing fraternity."

"Then there are a number of attractions which might have drawn them into the adventure of horse racing for the same mutual purposes. They might well have invested money in the same stud farm, or even a particular jockey or trainer, before stating their intentions to withdraw their cash to whoever was the recipient of their investment."

"A recipient who might well have vehemently objected to their request?"

"Yes, and was not in any position to return the monies paid so decided to kill them, or have them killed. On the other hand, it could be that they might well have formed a syndicate which frequently placed wagers at point to point meetings. It is fairly easy to run up large debts in such circumstances, which cannot be discharged without difficulty."

"The result being the ultimate punishment for not paying up?"

"Exactly Richard, but I do air on the side of caution my boy. I agree it does appear there existed some bizarre and singular characteristic which applied to each of them, but might not have been connected with their individual gambling habits."

"Some other motive unconnected with the turf do you think My Lord?"

"Yes, that is a distinct possibility."

The two men then spent some time discussing the intricacies involved in breeding and training high performance race horses, until Rayner had an in-depth knowledge of the sport.

Finally, after thanking His Lordship for sharing his knowledge, they shook hands and Richard Rayner took his leave, intending to return to Scotland Yard.

What the Inspector had learned during the past hour or so didn't really take his Investigation much further. However, having listened to His Lordship, his thinking was beginning to lean away from the murders having resulted from some financial connection with the turf. Other possible motives once again surfaced, including revenge for welching on a wager, but how would that be a reality unless all three had been acting in concert? Revenge was a powerful incentive for murder and yet the one man who might possibly have held such an entrenched grudge, Thomas Wake, was in the Inspector's opinion, not likely to have been the guilty party. The three handwritten messages left by the killer however, supported that theory.

As he walked up the stairs leading to his office, his thoughts were still wrestling with the kind of man who had committed all three murders. Then he realised there had been no fourth victim since he and Henry Bustle had visited the stables owned by Sir Samuel Grainger and Sir Neville Grimes. Could it be they had stirred up a hornet's nest, forcing the killer to go to ground for the time being? He gave that serious consideration.

Jack Robinson waited for the Inspector to hang up his top hat and coat. After sitting behind his desk and looking with interest across at the young Sergeant, he asked, "What have we Jack?"

"The name of one individual child who at some time attended all three workhouses sir," Robinson confessed, looking extremely satisfied with himself.

Chapter Nineteen

"A youngster by the name of Sidney Pitchfork spent time at the Christchurch Workhouse when Elias Thompson, the second victim was the manager there," Jack Robinson explained, "He was then transferred to the Cannon Street Workhouse during Conal Gumbley's tenure as manager, our third victim, and at the age of eight years, was again moved to the Upper Clapton Workhouse under the supervision of Claude Grimbold and his wife, the first of our victims."

After his brief report, the young detective stood facing Richard Rayner never before having felt such a sense of fulfilment and achievement. Jack Robinson had worked hard to present an extraordinary result which he knew was both impressive and extremely compelling to the Investigation.

"Well done Jack," an appreciative Richard Rayner

acknowledged, gently slamming the top of his desk with a palm, "Do we know what happened to the boy after leaving Grimbold's clutches?"

"According to their records, he was farmed out to Her Majesty's Navy to work as a powder monkey sir, when just ten years of age. But there is no trace of his name in navy records, which apparently isn't unusual."

The Inspector stood and stepped across to the fire, resting an elbow on the shelf above the hearth. He then enquired, "What of relatives or associates Jack?"

"There were none I could find sir. The boy was apparently an orphan and I couldn't find any note made of his parents."

"We therefore have a ten-year-old lad by the name of Sidney Pitchfork who appears to have suddenly disappeared into thin air. Perhaps one day his skeleton might be uncovered?"

"Do you really think so sir?"

"No, not really. I suspect that our ten-year old is a fully-grown man now Jack, and is either still living somewhere in London, or could have possibly been diverted away from the Royal Navy to take up a berth in the Merchant Navy, where it's also unlikely there would be any record of him in that service."

Rayner then reached for his hat and coat again, and invited

Sergeant Robinson to accompany him. Although the young man's exemplary investigative skills had just proven to be outstanding, they still had to trace the whereabouts of the individual he had discovered.

"Have you some idea where we might find Master Pitchfork sir?"

"No, but I might know a lady who could possibly point us in the right direction."

When they reached the Upper Clapton Workhouse, it was Nellie Prichard who answered the door and Richard Rayner begged to take a few minutes of her time. It was obvious the lady was anxious, looking back over her shoulder and quickly whispering, "The Madam is up and about. Go back down the lane from whence you came and you will see an inn called 'The White Cross', I will meet you in the back room there in just a few minutes." She then closed the door and her visitors left without further words being spoken.

It was a small inn which Rayner had noticed on each occasion he had visited the workhouse previously. After ordering drinks from a buxom barmaid with a heavily painted face, the two policemen retired to the small empty snug just off the corridor leading to the entrance.

"To put such fear into Miss Pritchard is beyond me Inspector," Jack Robinson confessed, "Mrs Grimbold must be an absolute tyrant to work for."

"It does seem that way Jack, but you know what, getting people to work through fear isn't the best way of obtaining the best you can get out of them."

"You should tell Superintendent Morgan that sir."

Nellie Pritchard suddenly appeared, wrapped in a shawl and Rayner offered to purchase a drink for the lady, but she politely refused, explaining that she couldn't be away from the workhouse for long.

"Then thank you for seeing us Miss Pritchard and I do fully appreciate your willingness to help us." The Inspector then mentioned the boy, Sidney Pitchfork to the lady, asking if she had any recollection of him during his stay at the workhouse.

She nodded and confessed that she remembered him well.

"A scrawny little fellow with fair hair and an angelic face," she confirmed, "He was another of those poor mites abused for no real reason, similar to young Thomas Wake, but not so frequently."

"Could you furnish us with more details?" the Inspector asked, "Was he thrown into the cellar like the other lad and beaten frequently?"

Nellie Pritchard looked extremely solemn as she described how Sidney Pitchfork was introduced to the birch on numerous occasions during his stay at the Upper Clapton Workhouse.

"He was constantly beaten until one night I found him whimpering in the dormitory, keeping the other boys and their mothers awake. When I attended to him, I saw the most horrific cuts across his poor back which were too severe to have been inflicted by a birch."

"Did the boy mention at the time who had harmed him in such a way, or what his punishment had been for?"

"No," she said, shaking her head, "He was too afraid, but I spent most of the remainder of that night I recall, tending to his wounds. I suspected he had been whipped by the master, Mr. Grimbold."

"Did you ever complain to either of them Mrs. Pritchard?"

"No, not on that occasion, but there was another incident I now remember when I found young Sidney Pitchfork hanging from one of the stalls inside the small stable at the back of the house. He'd had both his small thumbs bound together, which had then been lashed to a beam overhead and neither of his feet were touching the ground."

"My God," Jack Robinson spurted out in disgust of such treatment.

"Inspector," she continued, "The lad was unconscious when I found him on that occasion and I immediately took him in the carriage to a local doctor who complained most vociferously at the way in which the boy had been treated." She paused, thinking back to that devastating incident before explaining. "I mentioned that to Mrs. Grimbold and told her of the doctor's objections, but she turned on me and threatened me with instant dismissal if I ever again acted so unilaterally."

"Did she not ask how the boy was?" Jack Robinson enquired.

"No, that was of no concern to her, but I often wondered following that awful night what would have happened if young Pitchfork had died as a result of what they did to him."

"He would most likely have disappeared," Rayner suggested, "Were there ever any other similar incidents involving the same lad Miss Pritchard?"

"There were many Inspector. You see, it was always the same, not every boy was subjected to such severe ill-discipline, only the orphans who had no parents to fight their cause. It was as if both the master and mistress had an evil streak within them which required venting, and it was always one boy who was targeted, in a similar fashion to Thomas Wake."

"Did you ever hear of Master Pitchfork once he left the workhouse?"

"No," the lady said, again shaking her head, "I recall he was offered to the navy to work on one of their ships in Portsmouth, but I was so relieved he was finally escaping from the torture inflicted on him during the couple of years he had been with us. I didn't hear anything else about the lad after that."

"I am extremely grateful to you Miss Pritchard. Once again you have been a great help."

"There was one other thing I now recall Inspector. Sidney Pitchfork came to us I believe, from the Cannon Street Workhouse if my memory serves me right. And yet when he first arrived, I noticed even then a number of scars across his back from earlier floggings. He also had something wrong with one of his arms."

"In what way?" Rayner asked.

"It's difficult to remember, things are only just coming back to me as I speak about the boy. In some abstruse way his left arm lacked any power and used to hang by his side in a useless fashion."

"A consequence of his birth perhaps?"

"No, I don't think so sir. I believed at the time the boy's arm had been broken, causing some deformity as a result of him not having received the proper attention of a doctor. But he concealed it well and it wasn't something that was prolific. I only noticed it by watching over the lad during his stay with us."

Again, the lady was thanked before being allowed to leave and hastily return to her employment, but Rayner remained at the inn for some time afterwards, not wanting to cause Nellie Pritchard any hardship from being seen with her.

"Tell me your thoughts Jack?" the Inspector asked, taking another gulp from his tankard of ale.

"To be honest sir, if I had been put in that same position at such an early age, I would never forget those who had made my childhood so violently traumatic."

"Enough to commit murder?"

"Oh yes sir, most definitely. I think even now I could quite easily inflict a great deal of harm on those who had been responsible."

When they returned to Scotland Yard, the Superintendent was pacing up and down the corridor outside his office, waiting to ambush his Detective Inspector. There was the usual anxiety in Frederick Morgan's watery eyes and he quickly informed Richard

Rayner there had been a complaint of harassment from Sir Samuel Grainger. It concerned the Inspector's conduct when investigating the horse theft from Sir Neville Grimes's stables.

"He's written to the Commissioner Rayner, making all kinds of allegations about you."

"What kind of allegations Superintendent?"

"I'm not aware of the details, but we are soon to find out. I am to take you upstairs to see Sir Edmund immediately."

As the two senior detectives ascended the stairs to the top floor, Morgan moved as though he had crawly spiders in his britches and his breathing sounded nervously laboured. Richard Rayner however, continued to reflect a state of utter calmness and indifference. When they reached the Commissioner's office, they found Sir Edmund sitting in an armchair at the side of a blazing coal fire, perusing through a folder of papers. After the two officers appeared, he placed the folder on the floor and stepped across to his desk to retrieve a sheet of paper, before returning to his chair. He then explained that he had received a personal letter from Sir Samuel Grainger which had arrived that morning.

"The letter represents a formal complaint about your behaviour Inspector. The man writes that during your visits to his home, you were insolent and aggressive, falsely accusing his son and daughter-in-law of larceny. He goes on to accuse you further of threatening him with arrest should he fail to pay the sum of one hundred guineas to Sir Neville Grimes. Furthermore, he claims you demanded the use of his transport to assist in returning a horse called Fleet of Foot to Sir Neville, after it had been discovered on nearby property not belonging to Sir Samuel."

The Commissioner then waited for Richard Rayner to respond, which he did so by just smiling and shaking his head.

"Your flippancy surprises me Inspector. Have you nothing to say about these allegations which are far from the accepted behaviour I would have expected from any of my officers, let alone you in particular."

"No sir. I have nothing to offer in rejecting such allegations, except to direct you to the evidence I collated during my stay in Cambridgeshire."

"What evidence Inspector? Explain yourself."

"It's all contained in my report submitted to the Superintendent, together with the statements taken from a number of witnesses by Sergeant Bustle."

"I have it here sir," Frederick Morgan confirmed, before

handing over the file earlier left on his desk by the Inspector.

The Commissioner kept his visitors standing whilst he read through the articulately written report with the utmost deliberation. Finally, having carefully read everything that had been recorded, he looked up and declared, "It is not befitting a Knight of the Realm to indulge himself in such malicious fiction, but answer me this Inspector, did you take the sum of one hundred guineas to Sir Neville Giles as payment of compensation demanded from Sir Samuel?"

"No sir, I only asked for the temporary use of one of his horse boxes to transport the stolen horse back to its rightful owner. I can produce a copy of the telegram sent afterwards to Sir Samuel confirming the victim of the larceny of the horse had accepted his offer of compensation and I took no further part."

"Then explain the reason why this lady, Emily Grainger, was not brought into custody if the evidence against her was so overwhelming?"

In normal circumstances, Rayner's discretion would never have been challenged, but where a formal complaint had been registered every decision taken was apt to be scrutinised, and he sighed before answering the question.

"I was of the opinion that there was insufficient real criminal intent behind the taking of Fleet of Foot, and that the lady had been involved in the belief she and her husband, the other suspect, were merely committing a prank."

"Some prank Rayner," Morgan remarked, "The horse is worth thousands."

"It was kept in good condition and obviously well looked after when Mrs. Grainger took us to where it was being kept." He looked pleadingly at Sir Edmund and admitted he had probably made a mistake in not taking any further action, but truly believed the interests of justice were best served by the whole affair being treated as a civil matter.

"You erred Inspector, but what of the lady's husband, why was he not brought to book?"

"As soon as he was told we were looking for him, the man, Roland Grainger, went to ground and by then I did not warrant it beneficial to spend more time there, when our main Investigation involved the three murders here in London."

"Well, I give you fair warning Mr. Rayner, if a similar complaint, falsely made or otherwise, should come to light again, the consequences will be dire. On this occasion I shall reply to Sir Samuel Grainger and appraise him of the only action I believe deserved criticism, was your failure to arrest his son and daughter in law."

"Thank you, sir."

The Commissioner looked sharply at Rayner and abruptly said, "No Inspector, do not thank me. It is only your past record that has prevented me from taking the matter further." He paused before adding, "And the fact I believe what you have told me."

Both Inspector and Superintendent nodded their acknowledgements before leaving, and as they returned to the floor on which their offices were located, Morgan turned to Rayner and claimed, "You were lucky he was in a good mood."

"Do you really think so?"

Chapter Twenty

To those unfortunates who worked for and knew Gladys Grimbold well, she was a strong woman who frequently projected a merciless and mean streak, lacking compassion or understanding. Therefore, many were surprised by her bewailing response to the news of her husband's death, obviously feeling the severity of the repercussions of the tragedy. Apart from missing his robust companionship, it was also the circumstances of his untimely ending which had unnerved the woman. Even more surprising was Mrs. Grimbold's preference to take to her bed, remaining in isolation for a number of days. It was a different woman who eventually decided to leave her room, having regained some of the confidence lost through the bitter process of mourning.

When appearing at the breakfast table, having decided to put an end to her self-imposed retreat, the pale faced, emaciated woman sat with a straight back, weakly barking out her orders to the staff. Self-indulgence of any kind was an offensive trait of an individual's character, as far as she fervently believed. It seemed that self-denial was more important to the woman than good health or happiness.

It was Nellie Pritchard who suggested the mistress leave the house for a short walk to take advantage of fresh air for the first time in well over a week.

"I intend doing just that Miss Pritchard," Gladys Grimbold announced, sharply and before complaining about the delay in serving the porridge by the maid.

Although her employer gave the impression of an effete woman, compared with how the mistress had behaved over previous years, the Housekeeper still regarded her with trepidation. Following breakfast and putting such feelings to one side, Nellie Pritchard assisted the mistress with her coat, suggesting she also made use of a woollen cape to protect her from the early morning chill. It was the younger woman who insisted Mrs. Grimbold did not venture out alone until her strength was fully restored, before escorting her through the front door.

The two ladies walked slowly down the path until reaching the lane which was surrounded by open fields on either side, both intending to reach the nearby village of Upper Clapton before turning back. Nellie offered her arm for her companion to take as a means of support, but her invitation was refused with a short grunt and defiant shake of the head. That was until a cock pheasant suddenly leapt out of a hedgerow immediately in front of them, causing both women to start before the bird disappeared through an opposite hawthorn hedge.

Still, they continued with their walk and the frail looking workhouse mistress remained unsteady on her feet, trying hard but unable to shed the recent memory of her grievous loss. Her companion was tempted to mention the name of the boy, Sidney Pitchfork, Richard Rayner had quizzed her over on the day before. However, it was not the time, when there existed a distinct possibility of driving the woman back into the clutches of her ailing nervous disposition.

When they reached the village, Gladys Grimbold decided to go to church, so both ladies made their way up the narrow path leading to the small hill top stone-built chapel. They were the only participants of religious worship present and sat for a short time in the pews engaged in prayer, with the mistress requesting her worldly preferences to the Almighty, in a quiet but audible voice.

Finally, they decided to return to the workhouse and began to slowly retrace their steps from the village, in the opposite direction in which they had earlier walked. There were few people abroad and the odd one or two who enquired as to Mrs. Grimbold's health were acknowledged and thanked by Nellie Pritchard. It was then, after leaving the village behind them and where no other person was visible, they suddenly heard the trotting hooves of a horse approaching from behind. Both women turned to see a small enclosed carriage heading their way with a nondescript driver holding the reins.

For whatever reason, Nellie Pritchard's internal alarm bells began to ring and she became so instantly fearful her legs were unable to move. The horse drawn vehicle stopped at the side of where the two women were standing. The driver, who was wearing a heavy cape and hood across his head, moved with the speed of a Giselle. The intruder leapt from the top of the carriage and struck the immobile Gladys Grimbold across the head with some kind of heavy cudgel. No words were spoken as the injured woman collapsed to the ground with a groan, and her younger companion lapsed into shock, before fainting.

When Nellie Pritchard eventually re-joined the land of the living, she found herself spread out on the damp grass verge.

Both the horse and carriage had disappeared; so had the feeble frame of Gladys Grimbold.

When Richard Rayner and Frederick Morgan arrived at the workhouse, they found the Housekeeper resting on a sofa in a downstairs room with a maid and local doctor in attendance. She still appeared to be in shock, although her eyes welcomed the sight of the Inspector stepping into the room.

"Do not overtax her gentlemen," the elderly doctor instructed, "She has experienced a nasty ordeal and I have given her a sleeping powder. What she needs now is complete rest to aid her recovery." He then left with the maid who curtseyed before following him out of the room.

"I am so sorry to hear of your frightful experience," Rayner offered, crouching down and gently holding one of Nellie Pritchard's hands and introducing Superintendent Morgan. "Do you feel strong enough to briefly tell us about what happened Miss Pritchard?"

The stricken woman nodded and continued to relate her story.

"After coming to, I made my way back, only God knows how I managed to do that. There was no sign of Mrs. Grimbold so the man must have taken her off, but from the force of the blow he struck, she would have been severely injured if not killed."

"Bleedin' hell Rayner," Morgan gasped, before apologising for his verbal slip to the stricken lady.

"Can you describe your assailant Miss Pritchard?"

"He appeared to be a youngish man from the speed in which he moved, but I couldn't see his face. It happened all so quickly and he was wearing a black hood over his head which covered his face."

"Did he speak?"

She shook her head.

"Can you remember anything about the carriage he was driving?"

She thought for a moment and then described a black carriage, enclosed and pulled by a chestnut horse and that was all she could recollect.

"And you have no idea where he would have taken Mrs. Grimbold?"

"No Inspector, I fainted after seeing him strike the mistress, thinking I was about to be subjected to the same violence." Her eyes were beginning to well up, but then her voice began to slur as she tried to explain just how much terror she had felt. Richard Rayner noticed the woman's eyes were quickly becoming heavy. Very soon the sleeping powder would begin its work.

"Rest now Miss Pritchard," he suggested.

"God knows what he will do with her," she whispered, before slowly falling into unconsciousness.

The two detectives left the room and the Inspector instructed the maid who was waiting in the hall to attend to her mistress and ensure she wasn't disturbed.

Again, the maid curtseyed and watched the visitors leave through the front door.

"I wouldn't give much for the abducted woman's chances Rayner," Frederick Morgan remarked, as their carriage took them back to Scotland Yard.

"He picked his spot to take her after some careful planning," the Inspector answered.

"What makes you say that?"

"Because it was no coincidence he just turned up at the time when his victim just happened to leave the house, which tells us he must have spent a great deal of time waiting for her to appear."

"If you are right, and I happen to agree with you, that surely means our man was known to his victim."

Rayner then called out to their driver and instructed him to return to the village. As the transport slowed to turn in a 180-

degree circle, Morgan suggested that both abductor and abducted would be well away from Upper Clapton by then.

"I'm not so sure Superintendent. We are dealing with quite an audacious man and anything is possible in the way in which his mind works." But Frederick Morgan was proved to be right, as they found no sign in the village of the man or his horse and carriage, and a visit to the small chapel earlier visited by the two women, proved to be a fruitless exercise.

After eventually returning to Scotland Yard, arrangements were made for constables to be drafted into the area surrounding Upper Clapton. A widely spread search was quickly instigated for the missing woman and her kidnapper, the same man they suspected of having already murdered three of his victims. As evening began to approach, no sign of their quarry had been found and the Superintendent decided to hold another briefing in his office.

"I fear that we shall never see the woman alive again," he told Richard Rayner, who remained silent.

Jack Robinson suggested that particular attention should be concentrated on park benches and the entrances to theatres throughout the capital.

"How many men do you think we've got Robinson?" Morgan

scornfully said, "Those we have got are all out in the bleedin' sticks already looking for the woman."

"I do suggest we post a constable at the workhouse though," the Inspector suggested, "Just in case Mrs. Grimbold is returned there, although that possibility I must confess is a remote one."

"I agree Rayner," the Superintendent acknowledged, before sending Jack Robinson downstairs to inform the duty Inspector of the requirement.

Henry Bustle had remained extremely quiet up until then and Richard Rayner enquired as to any progress the Sergeant might have made in compiling a background record of Roland Grainger. He was still irked by the manner in which the young man's father had made an official and fictitious complaint about him to the Commissioner. Rayner had been trying hard to work out some logical reason behind such a course of action, and could only accept it had been an attempt to prevent his son from being arrested in the future in connection with the horse theft. The fact that the Inspector had made it quite clear he would be taking no further action had obviously been dismissed by the race horse owner, which had surprised the detective.

"My main source of information has been the local curator at Cheveley Parish Church sir," Bustle explained, "Whilst trying to be helpful, the elderly man is one who becomes easily confused and its proving to be quite an ordeal in trying to search through his records."

"In what way Henry?"

The Sergeant shrugged his shoulders and continued, "Well it's like this, he eventually found the record of Sir Samuel's marriage to one Mary Poulton who is now Lady Grainger, and also that of Roland Grainger's marriage to Emily Wake, but he failed to produce any record of the son's registered birth."

"Could it be that Roland Grainger's birth was registered in another parish?" Morgan suggested.

"I put that to him, but he insisted if that had been the case, the curator at Cheveley would still have had to have been informed at the time because that is the seat of the family home. But I intend returning tomorrow and persevering."

Jack Robinson then reappeared in the doorway and with some excitement in his voice announced that the missing Gladys Grimbold had been found.

"She was discovered by the local vicar sitting upright in one of the pews inside the chapel sir," he announced, "I'm afraid she is dead."

It was late by the time the small entourage from Scotland Yard arrived in the village and found a small group of local parishioners gathered outside the chapel, holding flaming torches with the vicar amongst them. Two constables had been diverted away from the search party to secure and protect the scene and Richard Rayner was first through the entrance, together with Frederick Morgan.

The victim was, as Jack Robinson had described earlier, sitting upright in the front pew facing the altar. Her eyes were open, as if staring at the crucifix attached to the wall above the altar, and her face resembled white marble. Surprisingly though, and unlike the previous three victims, there was no sign of blood visible and Rayner noticed a blue tinge on the lips of the corpse. His first suspicion was that she had been asphyxiated.

"She'll be paying for her past sins now," Morgan remarked, as Rayner crouched over the body and sniffed at the woman's mouth, before closing her eyes. It was then they both noticed a meat pie resting on the wooden bench, next to where she was propped up in an upright posture.

"Our man's calling card," the Superintendent quietly confirmed, "Bleedin' hell Rayner, he must be a total crackpot."

"She's been doped," Rayner commented, before reading the

message attached in the usual manner to the bottom of the pastry.

'God loves sinners', were the handwritten words.

"We need to catch this bastard quickly and put a stop to this," Morgan said, stating the obvious and before looking towards the altar, apologising to the Almighty for his slip of the tongue.

The Inspector straightened and looked directly into Morgan's eyes, swearing an oath that Gladys Grimbold would be the last victim attributed to this particular callous killer, now popularly known as the Pie-man.

Chapter Twenty One

Richard Rayner spent the remainder of that evening and night alone in his office at Scotland Yard, analysing and considering every minute snippet of information obtained from the enquiries made so far. The Inspector recorded in chalk on his blackboard, every inclination and suspicion he had nurtured; every fact and every opinion thrown into the investigative cauldron. Following a process whereby he divided the more certainties from the lesser possibilities already known, he was able to compile a fairly accurate intelligence and events map surrounding each of the murders.

Sitting at his desk, he then made a handwritten sketch of a number of possible and definite characteristics he believed commandeered the killer's behaviour. Each individual aspect was tested by corroborating evidence and reliable information gleaned thus far, until, satisfied he had produced a fairly accurate profile of the killer, he sat back and took a deep breath. The Inspector finally knew the identity of the man he sought. The problem he now faced was more testing. He required further factual evidence before he could possibly make an arrest and secure a subsequent conviction.

The murder of any human being resulted without exception, in public uproar, but the unlawful killing of a woman in particular, would be viewed with a greater sense of aggravation. Although the Inspector was aware of the kind of harsh and possibly on occasions, cruel lady, Gladys Grimbold had portrayed in life, the vast majority of those who had never come into contact with the woman would be ignorant of those characteristics. The newspapers would inevitably be spurred into heavy criticism of Scotland Yard, as was always the case when crimes of that nature failed to be detected with some immediacy, but that was the last concern Rayner had at that time.

After leaving his work place as the night sky was beginning to welcome the dawn, he made his way home feeling physically drained, albeit his thinking process remained as sharp as ever. He was fortunate not to disturb Clarice and eventually dozed off until being awakened by a kiss on his forehead from his wife, before she was due to leave the house to attend at her own place of employment.

"I've told cook to leave your breakfast until you feel fit enough to go downstairs," she whispered in his ear. But by then, Rayner was already fully awake and refreshed sufficiently to begin another day of investigative progress.

A plate of eggs and pancakes helped to stimulate his senses and after attending to his ablutions, the immaculately dressed Inspector was sitting in his carriage, being driven away from the house. His driver was instructed however, not to take him to Scotland Yard, which was Rayner's first visit each morning. He needed to speak once again with the pathologist, Doctor Critchley at St Mary's Hospital, so his carriage headed in that direction.

As they journeyed across the city, the Inspector's mind continued to concentrate on all the relevant points he had identified on the blackboard the night before. A picture of the killer had emerged and grew stronger as each hour had passed by. And yet, Rayner remained convinced there existed a feature which had not yet been revealed, and which he was confident would help to convict the man responsible for the murders of four people. What that was, he had no idea and was being driven towards that theory by mere assumption and gut feeling.

By the time he arrived at the mortuary, Doctor Albert Critchley had just completed the post mortem on the fourth victim and the

Inspector joined him in the examination room in a state of avidity.

"What have we doctor?" he enthusiastically asked.

"A different set of circumstances from those in which the previous three victims met their deaths Inspector," the pathologist confirmed.

"Yes, I suspected that would be the case when making my own cursory examination yesterday at the scene."

"The cause of death was the same as the others, in that the victim's heart had ceased to function," the doctor offered, "But unlike her predecessors, this woman wasn't stabbed through the chest. I believe she was electrocuted to an extent whereby she suffered from heart failure."

"In a similar way to some of the others doctor?"

"Not really." The doctor then indicated the fingers of the right hand and commented on the burn marks around the finger nails.

"As you can see, the blemishes are far greater than those seen on the previous victims. There is also a degree of discolouration around the backs of both hands and below the eye sockets, which leads me to believe the victim was subjected to a far higher voltage than before."

"What of the blue discolouration on the lips?"

"You have an acute eye Inspector. That I suspect was as the result of something being held against her face, possible a pillow or scarf, which prevented her from breathing but not sufficiently to produce death. An electric current did that."

"You suspect that would have been deliberate?"

"Possibly and most likely, or the woman's killer could have administered lower currents of electricity into his victim to cause as much distress as possible, before finally increasing the voltage sufficient to stop her heart."

"What kind of callous bastard would do such a thing?" Rayner asked. It was more of a comment than a question.

"The kind of callous bastard who appears to be making fools of the police Inspector, and is obviously intent on continuing with his agenda of death, at least for the time being."

"The obstruction placed on her face could very well have been used to keep her quiet during the time the man was indeed electrocuting his victim."

"I would agree that is highly feasible."

"Thank you doctor."

During his night time vigil at the blackboard, one of the outstanding queries which remained a concern to Richard Rayner had been the apparent absence of Roland Grainger's registration of birth. Such a feature had aroused the Inspector's suspicion, placing Sir Samuel Grainger's son at the top of his list of suspects.

After leaving the mortuary, he instructed his driver to take him to Somerset House where the General Register Office was based in the North Wing of the building. Once there, he spent the next few hours searching through the colossal number of public records maintained, helped by some assistance freely
given by a young blandly dressed clerk.

Finally, and having satisfied himself that the detour had been worthwhile, Rayner returned to Scotland Yard.

"I will not enquire as to where you have been Inspector," Superintendent Frederick Morgan said, perched in Rayner's seat, "Suffice it to say, I have no doubt it will be connected in some way with yet another academical and theoretical supposition of yours."

"Theorising based on facts Superintendent can be highly successful. It's called criminal investigation and I recommend it to you sir."

"Don't be impertinent Rayner," Morgan snapped back, hoisting himself out of the Inspector's chair to occupy another near to the door, "Life is difficult enough having to abstain from a bowl full of tobacco. But enough of the frivolity, when are you going to capture this bastard who's making monkeys out of us. Please tell me you have at least the slightest inkling of how the investigation is going to progress."

Richard Rayner smiled and looked across at the Superintendent mischievously before declaring, "I intend arresting the killer within the next few hours. Would you like to place a small wager on that claim sir?"

Morgan's face lit up, but his eyes remained wary, knowing that his Inspector wasn't the kind of man to make absurd nonsensical comments. Neither was he a betting man, unless his favoured option was an absolute certainty.

"Who is it then?" he demanded to know.

"What of the wager first, a pound, five pounds or perhaps even ten pounds Superintendent? To quote that well known saying, put your money where your mouth is...sir?"

"There will be no wager Rayner, now tell me who the bloody hell it is."

"There are two of them, two revengeful young men who have been collaborating with each other. And yet I suspect the principle party to the alliance, the killer himself, is one Sidney Pitchfork, who Jack Robinson revealed was in attendance at all three of the workhouses when managed by our three male victims."

"Who the bleedin' hell is Sidney Pitchfork, and where did his name come from?"

"I've just told you but he is better known to us as, Roland Grainger, an orphan who was adopted by Sir Samuel Grainger and his good lady when a mere twelve-year-old lad."

"Can we evidence that, Rayner?"

"Yes, I have a copy of the formal adoption record, obtained from the General Register Office, with a great deal of appreciation to Clive."

"Who the bleedin' hell is Clive, Roland Grainger's accomplice?"

"No, he's the clerk who has just assisted me in searching through the records."

"So, who is the second person associated with young Grainger?"

"I would rather keep that name to myself for now Superintendent, until I have more evidence to substantiate my suspicion."

Morgan looked at the Inspector with a doubtful eye and warned, "If you have got this wrong Rayner, you know exactly what will happen, following the complaint this Sir Samuel made against you? I take it you are prepared to put your career at risk?"

"It's because of his son's guilt, the man complained in the first place."

The Superintendent nodded his understanding and then asked, "When do you intend making your arrest?"

"Tonight, I shall take Sergeant Bustle with me back to Cambridgeshire and see if we can pay a surprise visit on that mysterious and enigmatic household."

"Just tread warily Rayner," Morgan cautioned, before turning towards the door, "I must inform the Commissioner, he's being put under a tremendous amount of pressure at the moment by those scavengers from the newspapers. I just hope and pray you have got this right."

"If I haven't Superintendent, I shall undoubtedly be joining the soup queues tomorrow," the Inspector joked.

As they headed for the south east of the country, being jostled to and fro as a result of the carriage wheels seemingly finding every carved-out rut in the thoroughfare, Rayner updated Henry Bustle on what he had discovered thus far.

The Sergeant was taken a little by surprise, especially when his Inspector listed all the pieces of information that pointed to his suspicions being factual.

"The fact that Roland Grainger is Sidney Pitchfork is reason enough to arouse our interest in the man Henry, but coupled with the fact the same man attended all three workhouses is, I suggest, quite fundamental."

"I agree sir, but what made you first think of Sir Samuel's son being the killer?"

"You remember the maid, Mavis Jennings, mentioned that she recalled a sweet smell coming from the same man who volunteered to take the stable boy's supper to him.?"

"Yes, she also recollected seeing him previously at the village dance."

"That she did. Well, she believed it was lavender water and when we were in Sir Samuel's library there was the distinct odour of lavender water in the air and I was aware that Lady Grainger didn't make use of such perfume, which made me suspicious that Roland Grainger was possibly the same man who called at Sir Giles Grimes kitchen that night."

"But what if the perfume came from Emily Grainger?"

"I didn't. I confirmed that when we spoke with her in the same room, prior to recovering the race horse."

Bustle nodded and then asked, "But how does that link in with the murders?"

"The same aroma could be detected inside the smoking room at the Royal Albert Hall, where Claude Grimbold's body was discovered. At first, I was prepared to accept one of the lady members of staff had been in there, but then having ascertained only Mary Marchant had entered the room and was not wearing lavender water, guessed it might well have come from the killer. We now know it most definitely did."

Again, Henry Bustle nodded his understanding and then asked how Richard Rayner intended carrying out the arrest inside Sir Samuel's house, knowing there would be opposition and objections made to the officers. He would be surprised if they were even allowed access without a magistrate's warrant.

"I agree with your sentiments Henry, and I'm not sure how to achieve our object just yet, but first we need to know that our man Roland is inside the house before making our move. I think we shall cross that bridge once we arrive there."

By the time they stopped at the livery in the village of Cheveley it was dark and, although the stable doors had been left unlocked, the old hostler had long left beforehand. Henry Bustle saw to their horse's needs, leading it inside to a suitable stall with the carriage remaining outside, close to the front of the wooden structure. After providing a bucket of fresh water, the Sergeant filled the manger attached to the wall, whilst Richard Rayner completed a brief note to be left for the hostler to that effect. The short missive also explained they would return to pay for the horse's overnight keep in the morning. Once satisfied the horse was settled, they left, closing the stable doors behind them.

Their surroundings appeared different in the darkness of night, with various landmarks appearing a lot vaguer than was the case in the fullness of daylight. The two detectives wasted little time in progressing towards where the Grainger estate was situated, and the stables soon came into view with the outline of the house in the background. All was quiet and the buildings were in total darkness. The incline leading up to the front door continued away from the main drive towards a copse of trees at the side, and it was there that Rayner stealthily led the way.

Once the detectives reached their covert position, they could see both the front and back of the house and Henry Bustle repeated his earlier question, speaking in a subdued voice. He already realised what his Inspector had in mind.

"How to do you intend we should take our man?"

"In handcuffs Henry," Rayner answered flippantly, "But first we have to find him and I believe the best way would be to sit and wait for him to appear. After all, if Roland Grainger is the same person we have been seeking then we only have a sketchy description of him from Miss Jennings."

The Sergeant pulled up the collar of his coat and leant against the trunk of a tree, knowing it was to be a long and fairly cold night.

"I suggest you try and rest awhile Henry for a couple of hours and then you can take over from me," Rayner said, never taking his eyes away from dark outline of the large house just a couple of hundred yards away from where they were hidden.

Then the sound of an owl hooting as it flew around in search of prey could be heard close by.

"There's a fat chance of getting any sleep with all that din going on," the Sergeant complained, before sitting down on some fallen bracken and resting his back up against the base of the same tree trunk. A few hours of snoring followed for the remainder of the night.

Chapter Twenty Two

The darkness had already given way to the early morning grey when Henry Bustle was awakened by Richard Rayner. He slowly got to his feet feeling every muscle in his body complaining.

"You let me sleep on sir," he remarked, appreciatively.

"There's some movement outside the front of the house, pull yourself together now Henry, we might have to move quickly," the Inspector directed.

Both men remained in their covert location and watched one of the stable boys climb down from an open carriage, which Rayner had just seen heading towards the house from the stables area. The lad then quickly walked to the back of the building out of sight and towards where the kitchen door was situated.

Bustle looked down towards the stable yard and commented that there was no sign of the usual riders and trainers about to take the horses out for their usual morning exercise.

"They've already been and gone," the Inspector told him, "But no one has yet left the house."

They continued to watch as the light improved and after a few minutes, saw the same stable boy leave the back of the house and return to the horse and trap which had been left standing outside the front door. The boy climbed back up on to the front seat and waited patiently, with both hands tucked inside his armpits and his head bowed as if about to fall asleep.

The observers remained watching the stationery transport for a good five minutes before a man appeared through the front door, wearing a grey cloak and soft cap with a pair of shiny black leather riding boots. He was carrying a small valise in his right hand.

Rayner strained his eyes and could see the same individual had a goatee beard. The Inspector concentrated on the way the man carried his left arm, remembering what Nellie Pritchard had earlier said about Sydney Pitchfork's deformity, but there was no sign of anything unusual, visible from where he stood.

"That looks like our man, Henry," he quickly suggested.

Both detectives then broke cover and ran down the incline, as the open carriage turned with the man from the house sitting next to the stable boy who was handling the reins. Slowly the vehicle moved along the lane leading to the village.

The pursuers were in luck only because the horse was kept at a steady walking pace and both detectives were in full flight. Richard Rayner was the first to reach the two travellers, shortly after losing sight of the house. In fact, neither of the individuals perched at the front of the open carriage saw him or the Sergeant speedily following their tracks. After running past the transport, surprising their quarry, the Inspector managed to grab the horse's bridle as the stable boy, not really knowing what to do about the intervention, pulled back on the reins bringing the vehicle to a standstill.

The man ordered the boy to keep moving and in response, Rayner produced his loaded pistol and pointed it in the suspect's direction.

"Remain exactly where you are," he loudly directed, as Henry Bustle finally arrived at his side.

"Mr. Roland Grainger I do believe?" Rayner spoke confidently, as he moved closer to the man and boy. He recognised the younger of the two as being the stable boy, Nicholas.

"Who in Dickens's name are you?" Grainger demanded to know, "We are not carrying any money with us," he declared upon seeing the Sergeant also approaching him, and being quite justified from Bustle's facial features to suspect the intruders had villainous motives.

"Do I look like a robber sir?" Rayner enquired, feeling a little insulted that his quarry would think such a thing.

"This is the detective from Scotland Yard sir," young Nicholas informed him.

"You will carefully step down from there Mr. Grainger," the Inspector ordered, still aiming the barrel of the gun at his man.

Grainger seemed to hesitate and then grabbed for the reins being held by the lad, but before he could take possession, Henry Bustle leapt up on to the back seat of the carriage and disabled the would-be fugitive by tightly wrapping an arm around his neck. The Sergeant jerked him backwards, pulling the wanted man over a wooden board separating the front of the vehicle from the back. A pair of heavy handcuffs briskly secured Roland Grainger's hands behind his back, resulting in vociferous and constant protests.

"Thank you, Henry," Rayner said, before climbing up to sit next to young Nicholas.

"Now you may proceed," he directed with a confident smile.

"Where to sir?" the youngster asked.

"Why, to the village of course."

During the short journey back to the livery, there was the

occasional verbal objection overheard from the back of the carriage, together with the sound of a sharp smack in the face. By the time their own carriage came into view, there was total silence from the back seat.

Few people were about at this time of the morning and the odd one or two local villagers could be seen making their way to their jobs of employment. They paid little attention to the group of travellers entering the village. The hostler was in attendance though, standing in the open doorway as the men from Scotland Yard arrived with their shackled prisoner.

During the time their horse was being led out to be harnessed to the official police carriage, Richard Rayner turned to young Nicholas and instructed the lad to leave the Grainger transport at the livery. He then told him to walk back to inform Sir Samuel that his son had been arrested for serious incidents in London. The boy nodded and made off back towards whence they had come.

The Inspector then turned to the hostler and after paying for their own horse's board, requested that the old man kept possession of the transport they had just arrived in until someone from the Grainger stud called to collect it. It was then time to leave for London and with Henry Bustle on top driving the covered carriage, Rayner remained inside sitting with the prisoner.

The morning sunshine bathed the surrounding countryside as the miles passed by, the scenic beauty attracting the attention of Richard Rayner. The prisoner strangely responded to his incarceration with long periods of silence, one side of his reddened face swollen as a result of the Sergeant's heavy hand striking home earlier. Roland Grainger's eyes never ceased to gaze out at the open fields and clusters of small cottages, as the carriage progressed towards the country's capital. However, the adopted son of Sir Samuel Grainger wasn't admiring the surrounding countryside, his mind concentrating only on the reasons why he had found himself sitting there handcuffed. Finally, as if suddenly being awakened from a deep trance he looked across at Richard Rayner and asked, strangely ingenuously, the reason for his arrest.

The Inspector however, was not fooled by the man's casual indifference and merely replied that he, Master Grainger, was already aware of the reasons for his detention.

"It must have been a living nightmare for you as a child?" Rayner genuinely asked.

"Pray tell me, what was?" the shackled prisoner enquired,

maintaining his look of a man who had been so dreadfully and unexpectedly wronged.

"The tortuous occasions you were made to spend with people who so gravely abused you Master Grainger, or should I call you by your given name of Sidney Pitchfork?"

The name appeared to strike a more devastating blow to the prisoner than anything Henry Bustle could have physically produced. His eyes widened and his facial features were suddenly set in stone. His mouth lay for a period slightly open and he just stared back at his captor in utter disbelief.

"The name means nothing to me," he then quietly and insincerely suggested.

In reply, Rayner smiled, but said nothing.

More miles passed by in silence, until Roland Grainger asked in a voice which croaked, "What evidence do you have that I am Sidney Pitchfork? My name is Grainger."

"By the fact you have just asked me that question," Rayner answered confidently, "And of course, there are still records to prove you were adopted by Sir Samuel and Lady Grainger when a mere twelve-year-old boy."

Again, a short period of silence followed. And then, most unexpectedly, Roland Grainger, alias Sidney Pitchfork, spoke with

285

a voice denoting a great deal of anger and passion.

"You could not possibly have the slightest idea of what it was like at the hands of those primitive barbarians. Tell me sir, have you ever felt the pain of a truly empty stomach, not for a day or two, but for weeks, only to be lashed across your back by a whip or stick when you had what was deemed to be the audacity to ask for food?"

"No, I have never been so unfortunate."

"Have you ever been left alone as a petrified child in the darkness of a freezing cold cellar for days and nights, until you can no longer feel any part of your body, only then to be carried out like a corpse and sexually interfered with?" There were tears in the prisoner's eyes.

Rayner's surprise at such a statement was obvious, and he actually winced at the very thought of what Grainger had just told him.

"I have," the man in handcuffs continued, "On more than several occasions. To them I was just a piece of garbage to be disposed of, and when it suited his perverse moods, I then became an object of his aberrant and unnatural sexual desire."

"I take it you speak of Conal Gumbley, the Administrator of the Cannon Street Workhouse?"

"I was an eight-year-old innocent boy when that filthy drunk first laid his hands on me, and I have never been able to dismiss from my nightmares the occasions I was thrashed into silence having complained as best an infant could."

"And what of Claude and Gladys Grimbold? Were they active in abusing young boys in a similar fashion?"

Grainger bowed his head and shook it vigorously, before once again looking up and across at the Inspector, the tears now falling down the side of his contorted face.

"In the whole of my life I have never asked for anything from any other man, woman or child; no charity; no favour; not even respect, and yet I was the innocent recipient of treatment which frequently pushed me to the very edge of escaping such deprivation by taking my own life, and all before I attained the age of ten years. Think on that Inspector."

"Were you ever sexually assaulted by Claude and Gladys Grimbold?" Rayner again asked, repeating his question.

"No, they just took satisfaction by beating and torturing me whenever such brutality took their fancy."

"And during the time you spent at the Christchurch Workhouse under the care of Elias Thompson, were you ever sexually abused there?"

"Thompson was a monster of the first order. He cared for nothing except to vent his twisted and bullying tactics on helpless children like myself. Would you believe that on one occasion that bastard actually chained me to a wooden post inside a shed, stark naked in the middle of January. Have you ever experienced that kind of trauma sir?"

Richard Rayner shook his head, finding every snippet of child brutality being shared with him, both daunting and discommoding.

"The memory of the pain I felt each time I struck that post with my head in an attempt to kill myself will haunt me for the rest of my days, but in answer to your question, no, Thompson never abused me sexually, which in a strange way might have been less cruel than laying his birch across my back several times a day."

Rayner sat back having listened to the man's recollections whilst sitting on the edge of his seat. He then confirmed without really considering the words he spoke, "I can fully understand now what drove you to avenge what they did to you."

The tears gave way to small fires in Grainger's eyes and he instantly spat back at the detective, "No matter what suffering I was able to inflict on those animals, it was insufficient to quell the anger I felt and still do."

Although the prisoner had confessed to each of the four murders to the Detective Inspector, Rayner had to remain professionally objective. It was necessary for him to remain unhindered by personal anger and empathy. His main concern was that once they arrived back at Scotland Yard, Grainger would not relent and go back on what he had said. In fact, when they finally stopped the first thing Richard Rayner did was to insist that Henry Bustle never laid a finger on the prisoner again. But Roland Grainger, the name now used by Sidney Pitchfork, had committed four gruesome murders in his quest for revenge, and would surely hang for his notorious deeds, no matter how mitigating the circumstances were.

As the prisoner was escorted to the cell block by Sergeant Bustle, Rayner returned to his office to be met by the Superintendent who was naturally impatient to receive an account of what had taken place in Cambridgeshire.

"You can rest easy Superintendent," the Inspector said, "We have the right man and there is sufficient to charge him with all four murders. Yet, there is still much to do, as I am finding it difficult to accept, he committed his crimes as a lone wolf."

"You still suspect there were others involved?" Frederick

Morgan asked.

"I am most certain of it and any accomplice needs to be put in the dock with our man, but as I said, there is still much to do."

"Have you any idea who that might be?"

"Yes, but I prefer to hold back on any suggestion at present."

Chapter Twenty Three

Sleep deprivation and the inability to think clearly, helped an extremely languid Richard Rayner to postpone any formal interview with Roland Grainger until the following morning. The Inspector was aware that a sharp mind would be required for conducting such a task, and his decision to go home was welcomed by Henry Bustle who could also take advantage by spending time with his wife and children.

Unfortunately for Clarice Rayner, the evening was spent isolated from any meaningful conversation with her husband, as the majority was spent with the man of the house asleep in an armchair. It was only when she and one of the maids helped the exhausted Inspector up the stairs to put him to bed, that he actually showed any signs of stirring. However, he slept soundly throughout the remainder of that night and was the first downstairs the following morning, completely re-energised with a mind as clear as crystal and an extremely healthy appetite.

Having been fully restored to his usual fervent enthusiasm, what Richard Rayner wasn't expecting when he finally returned to Scotland Yard, was a large group of newspaper reporters awaiting his arrival in the back yard.

"Is it right Inspector, you have arrested the Pie-man murderer?"

"What's his name Mr. Rayner? Can you tell us where he comes from?"

"Is it true, the story that the Pie-man has murdered other victims outside London?"

"Can you confirm he was a cannibal and has eaten some of his victims?"

The preposterous questions were thrown at him thick and fast and he was forced to push his way through the demanding human obstacle, before reaching the back door. If it hadn't been for the two constables on duty, preventing unauthorised persons from entering the building, Rayner was quite confident they would have actually followed him up to his office.

"Leave that lot to me," Frederick Morgan directed, as he was enjoying his first cup of tea of the day in Rayner's office, "I'll soon shift them." The one thing the Head of the Detective Branch was an expert at deploying was physical violence.

"I don't mind Superintendent, they are only doing their job, but I would appreciate no further interruptions throughout the morning."

Henry Bustle appeared shortly after the Inspector's arrival, threatening to punch the next reporter who accosted him.

"Strike them from your mind Henry, the Superintendent has promised to deal with the press and we have more important work to be getting on with," Rayner advised, as both men made their way downstairs to the cell block.

Roland Grainger sat in the interview room, grey faced and looking like a man who had only just realised the enormity of what his immediate future held in store for him. Although conscious his life would shortly be brought to an end by legal execution, the prisoner's remorse was limited to his own self-pity. There was a strong determination not to show any sympathy towards any of his victims. His glassy eyes were averted away from the two detectives sitting opposite him, preferring to stare down at the table top which separated the interviewers from the interviewee.

Richard Rayner began the proceedings by suggesting he would

discuss each of the crimes committed by the prisoner individually.

"I would rather not," a dejected Master Grainger offered, "I have confessed my guilt, is that not sufficient?"

Rayner nodded and then explained, "We need to take each matter further to clarify certain anomalies, beginning with the murder of Claude Grimbold whose body was discovered at the Royal Albert Hall. My question to you sir, is for what purpose would you leave your victim in such a highly regarded public place of entertainment?"

"As I have already explained Inspector, the consequences of the brutal and undignified treatment I was subjected to as a child rested heavily upon my shoulders throughout the years that followed." Grainger rolled his eyes up to the ceiling before continuing, "I suppose up until that moment, my lust for revenge had not reached a point whereby I felt any desire to end the lives of the culprits. I had always harboured the thought of causing them great pain, but I suppose death somehow seemed to be too good for them."

"Exactly what moment are you referring to?"

Grainger smirked nervously before continuing to explain, "When I first caught sight of Grimbold at a race meeting at

Newmarket I was attending with my father and one of his trainers, it was then all the hatred for the man surfaced. Memories of the past came flooding back to remind me of my detestation for what he had done to me. I was sickened by the sight of the creature standing there joyously taking his winnings from one of the bookmakers, and decided there and then he would pay for all the beatings and cruelty he had bestowed upon me. I felt a reprehensible desire to inflict upon him a debt of extreme pain and torture to be paid in full."

Henry Bustle continued to write down a record of every word spoken by the prisoner, having placed his usual three spare pencils on the table top.

"Pray tell me, what course of action did you take then?" Rayner calmly asked.

"I offered some excuse to my father for having to attend elsewhere and followed Grimbold until the man was about to climb on to his carriage." Grainger smiled at the memory he was relating to the detectives.

"At first he didn't recognise me, but when I told him who I was he squirmed and begged for forgiveness." The despotic confessor appeared to be enjoying his recollection.

"And did you or have you, forgiven him?" Rayner quietly

asked.

"No and I never shall. What he did was not worthy of mine or any other's forgiveness."

"I take it you then directed the man away from the racecourse at gun point."

The prisoner nodded.

"Why were you carrying a gun Mr. Grainger?"

"I was always armed when attending a race meeting, I suppose it was just in case we came across any undesirables, which you normally find at such events where a great deal of money exchanges hands."

"So, having your first victim within your grasp, where did you take him?"

Grainer hesitated and looked seriously back at Richard Rayner, before explaining, "I will tell all now Inspector as I have no other choice, but I cannot disclose where I conducted my private one to one confrontations with any of those who were the principle causes of my constant nightmares."

"Please continue."

"Once we were alone and I reminded him yet again of his foul practices, he begged for mercy, but I had none to give and beat him in an effort to have him taste some of the same punishment from which I was made to suffer. And then, having satisfied my own desperate desire for revenge, and when the time was appropriate, stabbed him through the heart, after ensuring he was well aware of what his fate was to be."

"So why leave his body at the Royal Albert Hall?"

"There was nothing more sinister than an overwhelming desire to leave the wretch in a public place, in the hope that his grotesque past conduct would become widely known. I knew a concert presented by Wagner would attract a full house so made my decision. That was the same with those who followed Claude Grimbold."

Henry Bustle stopped writing and asked a question of his own.

"How did you manage to get the man dressed in an evening suit before taking him there?"

"I didn't, he was already so attired when I first met him."

Rayner thought it strange a man would go to a race meeting dressed so formally, but decided not to press the matter. He had no reason to doubt what Grainger was telling him, except of course to protect any accomplice who might have been assisting him and which was the one obstacle he was yet to confront.

"I believe at some stage you used laudanum to induce calm to your victims. Was that how you managed to smuggle the man into the Royal Albert Hall?" Rayner asked.

"I used the same ether our veterinaries use on our horses when required, only to transport them to where I needed the privacy in which I could punish them. The laudanum was to keep them docile until I was ready to put an end to their miserable lives."

"But by having them drugged up to their eyeballs, how would they fully appreciate the full horror of what you did to them?"

"Oh, believe me, they all felt the full impact of the punishment I inflicted upon them, have no fear of that."

Again, the Sergeant stopped writing to ask yet another question.

"Why on earth did you leave a pastry with each of your victims, bearing an individual message attached to each of them?"

"Ah, you mean the meat pies," the prisoner answered, giving the appearance that it had been some kind of prank, "If you want the truth, I suppose it was a bizarre act sourced by a desire to mark those occasions when, as a child, I was made to endure periods of starvation. It was my way of reminding each of them the way in which I had been thrashed for merely asking for food."

"Even when they were dead?"

Again, Grainger smiled before explaining, "I stuffed each meat pie into their mouths and reminded them of their cruel acts, prior to killing them."

"And the meaning of the messages, written I presume in your own hand?" the Inspector enquired.

The man shrugged and quietly explained, "A way of feeding my own ego I suppose. I felt compelled to try and let the world know what each of those individuals were guilty of, and that was the only way I thought of communicating my feelings to you. If I could have written a more detailed script without identifying myself, I would have done so."

"And it was your own idea to do so?"

"Of course."

It was then that the Inspector noticed Roland Grainger's left arm appeared to hang down from his shoulder, and he enquired as the extent of the disability.

"It's not totally useless Inspector and has become a part of me. I broke it as a child and never received the treatment I should have done. The only way I have been impeded is the way in which my burden has prevented me from winning races."

Richard Rayner then consulted the folder of papers he had

before him, and allowed a few seconds of silence to pass whilst he searched for a particular passage contained in one of the reports. He then mentioned the killing of Elias Thompson, the man who Roland Grainger had earlier alleged tied him to a post in the middle of winter, stark naked.

"I take it you killed each of your victims at the same locations where they were eventually found?" he asked.

The man nodded.

"And am I right in saying that Master Thompson was taken to the Royal Strand Theatre having had laudanum administered to him?"

"Yes."

"Then how did you manage to get him inside the theatre after it had closed following an evening's performance?"

"I didn't. As with Grimbold, I had already taken him inside through a side door during the operetta which was being performed. Obviously, it was dark with the lights turned down, and we gave the appearance of two men looking for our seats, one drunk and the other helping him. By using such a guise, I awaited an opportunity to take him back stage, when no one was taking any notice of us. The performers there were too busy waiting to make their entrances to be bothered with a drunk and his friend, and I was able to hide us both in the props room, which was at the very back of the building. When the performance was at an end and everyone had left, all I had to do was remain hidden and allow Thompson to continue sleeping. Once I was satisfied there was no one left inside the theatre I woke him up and forced him to take a seat. He died in that same aisle seat and I have no regrets."

Everything the prisoner had told them was corroborated by the nature of the events which had taken place, and Richard Rayner had been surprised by the amount of detail shared by the man. He stood and stepped away from the table, leaning against a wall with both hands in his pockets, before pointing out that some of the young man's victims had in fact been electrocuted.

"Pray tell us the reason for using electricity in such a way it would cause a great deal of pain before their eventual deaths?" he asked, already knowing the answer but the question was a prelude to an intention to probe further.

"For the same reasons I whipped and beat them," the prisoner answered without hesitation.

"And you never thought that by doing so, you had become as wicked and cruel as your aggressors?"

Grainger hesitated to think before replying.

"I only felt complete satisfaction for what they had done to me. Again Inspector, try putting yourself in my position and you might understand more clearly."

"I understand Mr. Grainger clearly enough, I can assure you." Rayner could certainly understand the intense feeling for revenge at the time the prisoner was a helpless child, being subjected to such harsh cruelty. But not after such a lengthy passage of time since those vile acts of wickedness had taken place. By taking his revenge in such a way as he had just described, Roland Grainger had displayed the same signs of depravity as those he had been subjected to as an eight-year-old. He was looking for some hint of remorse from the man, but there was none to be seen.

"If you possess the slightest regret for your own foul deeds, you will tell us how and where the source which was used to electrocute those people is located."

Grainger just sat looking up at him with a stern and immoveable expression on his drawn face.

"Tell me about Elias Thompson, Conal Grumbly and Grace Grimbold. Why electrocute them when there was no indication of you having done so in Claude Grimbold's case?"

"Even I could not flog a woman and just felt that she owed me her life for having supported her wicked husband when committing his vile acts."

"Where is the machine you used, to be found Mr. Grainger?"

Again, the man said nothing in reply.

"Then I must assume it is kept in the same location where you inflicted your own methods of torture on each of your victims. It therefore stands to reason, you had an accomplice to assist you, someone who held the same revengeful lusts as yourself."

"There was no one," Grainger declared.

"I think you are lying sir?"

"Why should I? I've told you everything I know."

"Very well," Rayner said, moving towards the door, "Sergeant Bustle will return you to your cell and perhaps we shall talk more a little later." The Inspector then left the room and headed back towards his office. He met Frederick Morgan in the first-floor corridor.

The Superintendent enquired as to how the interview was progressing and Rayner informed him of the manner in which Roland Grainger had talked openly about his criminal deeds.

"But he refuses to tell us the location of the machine he used to electrocute his victims, or how he gained the knowledge required to use the thing."

"Perhaps I should go down there and introduce him to these,"

Morgan said, raising both his fists. He was a man of impatience and extreme violence and would no doubt have beaten Roland Grainger to a pulp, possibly extracting the identity of any accomplice from him. But Morgan's methods of interrogation were not the same as Richard Rayner's, and were generally deplored by the Inspector.

"No, I do not believe that would work. He's told us everything he could about the murders and the reasons behind them, but I believe he's shielding someone else and is determined not to inform us of their identity. I fancy another visit to the Lambeth Workhouse."

Roland Grainger's admissions and descriptive accounts of his murderous activities were still ringing in his ears, when the Inspector arrived at his next destination.

Violet Pudsey had been the Administrator of the Lambeth Workhouse for the past twenty years, having spent the previous ten years as the Housekeeper at the same establishment. She was an elderly, rounded woman with a large but warm and friendly face above a double chin. The lady's crown of greying hair signalled she was drawing closer to retirement.

"I understand you are interested in knowing about a former

inmate of ours Inspector?" she spoke in a local London accent.

"Yes, Emily Wake. Do you recall the girl? I understand she remained here until she was sixteen years of age?"

"Yes, a nicer girl you would never wish to meet. I also remember her brother but cannot recollect his name now. Unlike his sister, he was a disturbed young lad who my heart went out to, suspecting he'd been subjected to more than just chastisement."

"My enquiry is to confirm whether or not the girl was connected in any way with the subject of electricity Mrs. Pudsey. Do you recall anything at all which might have associated young Emily with such a subject?"

The woman looked away in deep recollection for some time, before answering Rayner's query.

"No, I cannot; but I do recall her younger brother constantly enquiring as to how the new innovation worked. Yes, I remember now, his name was Tommy and he seemed to become obsessed with the way in which various objects could be moved by applying currents of electricity to them, but it was all above our heads."

"Thank you, Mrs. Pudsey, that has been a great help."

Richard Rayner spent that following evening at home in the

company of his wife, but as was the case during the previous night, the Inspector was poor company. Determined to introduce more clarity to his suggested suppositions, he spent some time in his library, reading through one scientific journal in particular which was relevant to the various uses of electricity. His wife respected her husband's need for privacy so remained distant from him. Clarice was surprised when he began to make various sketches on pieces of paper.

Eventually, the lounge floor was covered with individual sheets containing a crude effort of recording what the front of each workhouse Rayner and Bustle had visited looked like, drawn entirely from his memory. The final sketch he made was of a wooden shed in a garden with some resemblance of small shrubs surrounding the structure and bordering each side of a narrow path leading to the shed. When that particular drawing had been made, Rayner sat staring at it before finally relaxing. He wished his wife a good night without further explanation, and retired up the stairs to their bedroom.

Chapter Twenty Four

Once again, the village of Cheveley beckoned and when the Scotland Yard detectives arrived, Richard Rayner drove the horse and carriage past the livery before stopping outside the front of the small cottage occupied by Thomas Wake. There was no response to Henry Bustle's loud knocks on the door, so the Inspector led the way around the side to the back of the quaint and peaceful domicile. He then stood for a moment observing the back garden which contained the wooden shed with shrubs bordering each side of a narrow path leading to the shed door.

Rayner found himself looking at the same scene he had sketched from memory the night before, when sitting in his own lounge. It was at that very moment, he became aware of the analytical mind he possessed having finally taken him to the brink of success.

"I think we are about to discover the location of the contraption we need to recover Henry," he quietly pointed out.

"In that shed sir?"

Rayner nodded before following the short path, as if being drawn towards a magnetic field. He noticed there were no windows through which to peer into the structure, which he considered was a positive sign. The singular door was locked and the Inspector stepped back before kicking it open with his highly polished boot.

The interior contained a few garden tools hanging from nails down one wall, but placed on top of a small table up in the far corner, was what appeared to be some kind of home-made machine.

Rayner examined the squared shaped wooden box-like object and could see a row of small switches with an array of knobs and dials running across the back. Protruding from the machine were four lengthy wire leads, each containing a metal grip on the end, and obviously used to carry currents from the generator. Protruding out of one side was a large handle, obviously required to activate the device by constant turning. There was also one solitary wooden chair positioned near to the centre of the floor, with leather straps attached to the back rest. That in itself convinced him they were standing inside a torture chamber, which had undoubtedly witnessed horrific events.

"I do believe we are standing in the same shed in which Master Grainger's victims were tortured and electrocuted Henry," the Inspector grimly suggested.

"Regretfully sir, I have a picture in my mind of how those unfortunate people must have suffered," the Sergeant said, pausing for a moment before continuing, "Our man's victims must have made a lot of noise during his macabre practices. I would have thought someone close by would have heard them screaming out?"

"Who though Henry? There is no one living adjacent to this property so who would there be to hear their cries for mercy?"

"My God, we certainly got this one wrong Inspector."

"So it would seem Henry. I fully accept responsibility for our distorted belief that Thomas Wake was an innocent party to all of this," Rayner answered, his eyes never diverting away from the grim appearance of the instrument standing before them, "But now we can only make amends and hope our bird hasn't already flown."

"I take it our first port of call will be the Grainger house and stables?"

"No, I think not. For now, we need to remain as concealed as we possibly can until we have our quarry within our sights."

Rayner was feeling some anger at the way in which he'd been so obviously duped by the professional jockey, and now feeling the edge, was determined to put matters right.

"What do you suggest sir?"

"There is good reason to believe our man is still hanging around in this vicinity. After all, he's due to ride in the Derby and unless he becomes aware that we know all about the role he has played in all four murders, there is no logical reason for him to disappear."

"It does appear that both Master Wake and Roland Grainger were acting in concert with each other, participating in the torture and electrocution of their victims, here in this very shed. It's enough to send shivers down your spine."

"I suspect there's more to what has taken place than we imagine. I believe that Wake and Grainger knew each other when they were mere children, possibly when staying at the Upper Clapton Workhouse, and I also suspect that when the two jockeys decided to take their revenge on Claude Grimbold, a pact was agreed between them."

"An agreement to murder each of those who had been responsible for their brutal treatment when they were children?"

"Without doubt Henry; revenge is a most powerful incentive to commit murder, but we must remain patient. I have every confidence that once we have the man in our net, Master Wake will describe the role he had played when dealing with all four victims."

"I don't think Sir Samuel Grainger will be overjoyed. He would have lost both his adopted son and first choice jockey for the Derby in just a matter of a few days."

"He will also be given the opportunity to stop harbouring two killers."

Rayner then realised their horse and carriage had to be concealed. The transport had to be moved away from the front of the cottage. Returning to their vehicle, they drove it back to the livery where they left it in the care of the hostler, insisting both horse and carriage remained out of sight at the back of the stables. When they returned on foot to the cottage, both were prepared for a prolonged vigil.

The wooden shed which they suspected had witnessed so many horrors was an ideal place from which they could observe the back of Thomas Wake's residence. The door was left ajar, sufficiently to see the whole width of the cottage and Bustle took up a position on the floorboards, whilst his Inspector took advantage of the only chair, ignoring the leather straps obviously used to have secured the captives.

Both detectives made a wager for a shilling; the Sergeant favouring their man would return to his home before darkness fell, and Rayner suspecting that Wake would not be seen until after dark. Following a lengthy and tedious wait, it was Henry Bustle who finally won the wager.

In the early evening dusk, they both saw some movement through the ground floor back window before a lamp was lit. The figure of the wanted man could be clearly seen striding across the room.

"He's gone in through the front door," Bustle confirmed, stating the obvious and holding out a palm to collect his one shilling winnings.

"Come Henry, let's not brook any further delay in notifying our man of our presence."

The Sergeant remained at the back of the cottage, whilst Richard Rayner quietly made his way unseen around to the front.

When Thomas Wake answered the door, he looked surprised to see the Inspector standing there. Rayner waited for an invitation to enter the cottage, but none was forthcoming, just a question from the jockey as to how he could help further. He was ignored and the Inspector boldly stepped past the suspect and entered the parlour uninvited. He was in no mood for niceties or trivialities and a bemused Master Wake followed behind him.

"I'm afraid I am at a loss at to why you have returned Inspector," he said, looking fairly calm and unnerved by Rayner's presence.

The man from London requested that the jockey unbolted his back door to allow his Sergeant to enter.

"He's been examining your shrubs out back," he sarcastically said, "Henry's always been a keen gardener you see."

The younger man remained confused but did as he had been instructed, opening the kitchen door with the Inspector staying close to him.

By the time all three had returned to the parlour, the occupier had lost some of his earlier calm composure and nervously asked, "Again, what is the purpose for this visit Inspector?"

Richard Rayner, who remained standing with Henry Bustle answered, "I have always had a fascination about electricity Mr. Wake and understand you also used to delve into the secrets of such an innovation?"

It was obvious from the look on his face that the race winning jockey was wondering whether the detectives were aware of what he had stored inside his garden shed, but decided to continue with his charade.

"Yes sir, I did once hold an interest for the subject but that was many years ago, when I was much younger."

"And you haven't undertaken any experiments with electricity more recently?"

"No, my mind is concentrated only on my next race these days Inspector, under the protection of Sir Samuel I might add."

Rayner thought the last remark was somewhat strange to make, or could it have been construed as a warning of some kind? It was of no matter though; words wasted on a man who was convinced he was facing a brutal killer.

"Then pray tell me sir, how do you explain the presence of a generator in your garden shed?" He was wondering why Wake had not made any enquiry about the disposition of his friend and brother-in-law Roland Grainger. It was obvious, being thirty-six hours after Sir Samuel's son's apprehension, the whole of the Grainger household would have known by now that Emily Wake's husband had been taken to London.

Richard Rayner's last question was the one the professional jockey had been fearing, as he had no legitimate answer to give. He just sat there, obviously considering his position and wondering what else Roland Grainger had told them.

"Well, we are waiting Mr. Wake. For what purpose do you require a generator, or shall I attempt to jog your memory sir?

The man just shrugged his shoulders and looked up from his chair with a vacant stare, still groping in the dark as to what these Scotland Yard detectives knew. He was soon to find out.

"By the way, Roland Grainger has been open and honest with us, disclosing all about the events with which he will be later charged," Rayner quietly explained, never taking his eyes off the younger man.

"That must make you a happy man then Inspector," was the only answer forthcoming.

"That garden shed out back is where yourself and Roland Grainger took your victims and tortured them, before finally bringing to an end their painful misery. Is that not the truth sir?"

At first Thomas Wake opened his mouth, as if to feign innocence and make a total denial of the accusation, and yet, he knew at that moment, all was lost. Roland Grainger must have talked to clear his conscience. Yet, Richard Rayner saw an immediate distinctive change in the man's eyes, from having been relatively concerned, to portraying a look of desperation.

"What has happened to Roland?" the distraught man finally enquired in a whisper, as if petrified someone other than the

London detectives would hear the sound of his voice.

"Master Grainger has admitted the role he played in each of the four murders, in an effort to escape the noose. Are you so minded sir?"

Wake rose to his feet and explained, "I want to show you something important Inspector." He stepped across the room to a chest in the far corner. Upon opening the top drawer, he dipped his hand inside, and Rayner immediately nodded at Henry Bustle. The Sergeant required no time in which to consider what his Inspector was suggesting, and without hesitation sprung at young Thomas Wake, grasping the arm belonging to the hand inside the drawer.

A loaded pistol was produced in Thomas Wake's hand and a struggle followed in which the firearm was snatched from the aggressor's grip and flung to the floor. Why on earth the professional jockey continued to flay his fists at such an experienced street fighter as Henry Bustle, alluded Richard Rayner, and he stepped back already knowing the outcome of the confrontation. The smaller of the two men became the recipient of a clenched fist which struck him hard on the side of the head, sending him flying over a chair. Such a singular blow was sufficient, although the Sergeant kept his fists raised to inflict further punishment if required.

"Enough Thomas; persistence will only result in more pain," the Inspector indicated.

The beaten man clumsily climbed back off the floor, before both hands were handcuffed behind his back, whilst Rayner recovered the pistol and made it harmless. He then stood for a moment of silence, facing Thomas Wake. The man was at his lowest ebb and more vulnerable to answering truthfully questions there and then, than he would have been by the time they returned to London.

"What I am interested in Mr. Wake is whether your sister, Emily, was involved in any of this?" Rayner quietly and calmly asked, knowing what effect the inference behind the question would have on their prisoner.

"No, that's a ludicrous idea, no matter what her weakling of a husband might have told you." It was the response the Inspector had anticipated, but Richard Rayner needed further convincing.

"Oh, I don't know so much. A man who can abduct three men and a woman before murdering them with a little help from yourself, I would certainly not describe as being a weakling." Rayner paused and watched as Wake's head dropped lower towards the floor, with Henry Bustle maintaining a strong grip on one of the man's arms.

"I have a mind to arrest your sister and take her back with us to London," the Inspector announced.

Once again, the prisoner raised his head and on this occasion was convincing.

"I will admit to all what I have done, without regret, but Emily knows nothing and it would be a travesty of justice if you were to involve her in the activities of myself and Roland Grainger,"

"Then I believe you Master Wake, but tell me this much. What role did you play in the abduction and murder of Conal Gumbley, the former manager of the Cannon Street Workhouse?"

"I didn't Inspector, that was a pleasure I left to Sir Samuel's son. How could I, when I was in your company at the time. In fact, I didn't participate in any of the abductions and that's the truth."

"Perhaps, but you most certainly took advantage of taking your own revenge by applying electric shocks to them, after Roland Grainger had brought each individual to you."

The man nodded, but said no more.

Before leaving for London that same night, Rayner requested the local constabulary to take possession of the generator and keep the cottage owned by Sir Samuel Grainger secured, until detectives could travel from Scotland Yard to make a thorough search of the property. The machine which had been used to cause so much pain and cruelty, was to eventually be returned to Scotland Yard as an important item of evidence.

Thomas Wake sat inside the carriage throughout the return journey to the capital, knowing that his life was nearing its end. The nightmarish memories and scars of a childhood in which he had suffered so greatly, remained and would do so when he stood on the trap door with the hangman's noose around his neck. Albeit, many would have felt he and his accomplice were justified in carrying out their revengeful acts and illegal executions, to have taken the law into their own hands in the manner in which they had done so, could only result in one course of action.

It was very late when their carriage finally arrived at the back of Scotland Yard and Henry Bustle quickly and quietly escorted their second prisoner to the cells before both men went home where they were to spend the remainder of the night.

The following morning, they met in Rayner's office, both refreshed and satisfied with their achievements of the past couple of days, although the incidents which had driven the killers calculated crimes of murder, negated any celebratory mood.

"Sir Samuel Grainger is seeing the Commissioner as we speak," Frederick Morgan confessed, "He is asking what we have done with his son and first choice jockey."

"Will Sir Edmund tell him Superintendent?" Henry Bustle asked.

"Of course, and he won't hesitate in informing the arrogant bastard that he was guilty of harbouring two killers, even if he unwittingly did so, but tell me," Morgan continued, turning to face Richard Rayner, "How in God's name did you know that this Thomas Wake had a generator in his garden shed?"

"Mere supposition Superintendent, until of course we saw it standing there. You can call it a detective's intuition if you like."

"Well, one thing is for certain," Bustle announced, "I won't be placing a wager of Green Eyes to win this year's Derby, not now it's lost its jockey."

"You and me both Henry," the Inspector said, stretching himself in readiness for a lengthy interview with Thomas Wake.

If you enjoyed reading this book, we recommend the following written by the same author:

About the Author

John F Plimmer studied Law and Philosophy at Birmingham University where he was awarded degrees in both subjects. Since then he has been a feature writer for both newspapers and magazines and been involved in script writing for a number of television's most popular dramas.

He is frequently involved in debates and commentaries on both television and radio and to date has over forty books published. Some of his works include 'Brickbats and Tutus' - the biography of Julie Felix, Britain's first black ballerina and Backstreet Urchins – a humorous account of life in the Birmingham slums of post war Britain.

The Dan Mitchell series involves international espionage and murder and his popular Victorian Detective Casebook series includes seven books describing the adventures of Richard Rayner and Henry Bustle of Scotland Yard.

Other published books in the Victorian Casebook series:

The Victorian Case Review Detective
The Graveyard Murders
A Farthing for a Life
The Bullion Train Robbery
Rayner's Ripper
The Fourteenth Victim
The Pie Man
25 Augustus Street

Printed in Great Britain
by Amazon